DOCTOR
PATHIC

ALEXANDER MACHISKINIC

Doctor Pathic
Copyright © 2021 by Alexander Machiskinic

All rights reserved. No part of this publication may be reproduced, distributed,
or transmitted in any form or by any means, including photocopying, recording,
or other electronic or mechanical methods, without the prior written permission
of the author, except in the case of brief quotations embodied in critical
reviews and certain other non-commercial uses permitted by copyright law.

Tellwell Talent
www.tellwell.ca

ISBN
978-0-2288-7096-8 (Paperback)

If the Big Bang had consisted of just atoms, the universe couldn't be infinitely hot and infinitely dense at the point of infinity, at the beginning. Atoms do not last forever because they have a half life, so they won't reach infinity—but they may portray it because atoms that have already melted down share their properties with the half life of other atoms, creating the illusion of infinity. They turn into molecules in a very short amount of time.

Models of this infinity can be seen in a black hole, but just a part of it, because a black hole's infinity is not like the Big Bang. It starts off with light bending in space, and then when it reaches the inside of the black hole, the light tucks behind the atoms that is the proportionate weight of the decomposing atom. When the atom reaches its point of decay, it falls behind another atom, creating a molecule that has a certain amount of time until it decays again. If it were to fuse, the atom would fall onto the gravity and the light would bend around the atom, falling into the black hole and creating the black illusion. Fission. You could see the atom at the sides of the black hole slowly falling apart if it reached half life, fusing if it was refused by its own properties, like the electron. Somewhere out in space, everything fused up into molecules some time after the Big Bang. Before the Big Bang, everything happened. I saw.

Space and Time

Time travel. Third Day,

In between time travel sequences.

Games. Molotov cocktails. I made a Molotov cocktail because I needed one for the games. If I didn't make a Molotov cocktail, I couldn't participate in the games. I did not want to participate in the games, and I wouldn't take orders anyway. In fact, throwing cocktails over was to signify the beginning of the games. If they started giving instructions, everybody ran because there were orders. And fallout could happen fast. Someone could catch the cocktail and just as easily throw it back.

In the beginning, the games weren't launched like that. They never promoted free will, but if you had a gold medal—first place—you made it in their charts. This is how you would see games being launched. One time, I threw the cocktail, and the games were on. I saw someone budge, so I left just as fast as I had a chance to escape, as this boy could get to me. And in these games, I never participated. I could have booked past them, but in order to make do in participation of the games, I kicked a man's door down and ran through. He saw me go in and chased me. I booked it through the back door and hopped a fence, looking behind me regularly to see if I was being followed. Once I lost him, I made sure I was seen by him coming back. I knocked on everyone's doors nearby so that they would all say that they'd seen me.

I wanted to be the best, so I ventured back through the back door of this old couple's house and found the boy. Before he could do anything, I took off again to knock on everyone else's doors in recognition of the games. So I called everyone, knocked on their doors, and ditched up the block to be seen by the first person, and last person, and then knocked on more doors. When they saw it could have been complete gibberish, I ran away from everyone after having pounded on their doors.

The games were on. Everybody was stealing and running away, slapping the bottle, slapping another's bottle and running, doing something cheeky and running. If someone wanted to do something to you, you could slap their cheeks so that they understood if they tried to restrain you lethally.

We were carefully instructed to throw the cocktail over a building to signify the beginning of the games. The games were made that way to signify the beginning. In the beginning there was peace, because there was nothing. Some might say that they were waiting for the Big Bang. Literally waiting. The games were perfect for the people who liked perfection. They made everything so that you needed to qualify. You could take a piece of the games with you during this fallout, with no supplies, if you threw the cocktail over your head. "That is to signify that there is no peace." No peace. If you had a cocktail, you could participate in launching the games. You could drink if you wanted to if you didn't use pure fuel in the cocktail.

They use Molotov cocktails for the games. We spied on them while working. You could see people training and getting buff and ready to compete, just like it said in the beginning. I left and threw a cocktail in significance of the games starting. I had no place to go because I wanted to follow the trainers, the ones getting ready for the games like the ones in the beginning, to see what games should really be like. They needed chaos or else they would sit in their seats rotting and cheering for straight-faced no ones.

It was the beginning of time, just before the Big Bang. There was infinite pressure and infinite density in a shape called a singularity. This left people waiting, even your ancestors. In reality, what led to your life began with your families, then your grandfathers, then your great grandfathers, then your ancestors, then your great ancestors, then their fathers and grandfathers, and all the way back to the beginning, even to fish and geckos, everything, until you went back to see the beginning.

In my life, I was playing when the Big Bang happened, and then I flew away. I lived on sacred land and worked out until I became like a shadow and strong as muscle. I let the muscle sink into my body and weave my bones, pure muscle, like a shadow. You could see my smile. I wasn't smiling, but those were my teeth.

Then, back in time, a flash from the Big Bang. Then sickness, and finally the perfect village. This flash right after the Big Bang lit up everything; imaginary stars were born, and un-imaginary ones were blown up from the quantum universe to be born in the future. We wanted space to look nice, sprinkled with stars, so we climbed up into the stars. We plucked dirt and clay from the ground and mixed this matter with lighter elements to make gunpowder. Then we lit up the land. The sky was dark, so we lit up the land.

Upon doing so, we shot into the flames to explode the land, and we shot at the fire to ignite a star. Upon ignition of this star, we blew up the land to chase after this star that needed much love to live the right way, in beauty. We then shot up the land to give rise to gravity; we were in freefall, much like many things in space.

When we shot up the land to blow up the planet, we slowly froze, and I only needed to flex to bring myself into rest, stasis, mummy. I had a limited amount of time, so I started myself to sleep and started seeing people. I did not like that, so I brought myself into concentration to think about what was in front of me. I thought about the land, and I saw a picture in my mind that showed what was outside that thought. If I ripped my mind out of stasis, I would see rot, and bugs crawling out of my skin from being a mummy. So I stayed asleep in the mummy to learn what to do.

I would remain in stasis because freezing a second time might hurt. I started dreaming. I wanted to turn over, and these were my thoughts. I said, "I have a body, but it is floating in stasis." I brought myself to hallucinate, and I saw someone. I had to concentrate to let him go from my mind. Etched into the mummy's body were instructions on how to bring yourself out of hallucinations. Then I said, "Am I in orbit, or am I somewhere to find myself, lost in exospace?" I was lost, but I noticed that I had a body. I was using it inside of my mind. Where did this body come from? It didn't come to me before I was born, and I must have passed out before I was born, just like death, because I didn't exist. I didn't see my deceased family members wake up in their coffins at the funeral. So sleep must be the final resting place, the forefront of death.

When I was born, I came from molecules my mother ate while I was in the womb, everything she gathered up from all over to feed me through my umbilical cord. I came from consciousness all around the world my mother ate, from foods being shipped as produce to be sold at markets. Everywhere. And like consciousness, I was born from consciousness in my mother's womb. Upon death, I would not be from gathered food from all over the place like you would in your mother's womb. Instead, you would put my body back where it came from, the opposite, if you happened to go this way. You would die from not taking care of your body. I would be spread all over the place while dying, and you would die from the opposite of prenatal care: no food, just you in a coffin. In reality, you should preserve your body. You should work out until all parts of your body dissolve into thin air. You should preserve your body. Working out until your body dissolves is where you should take yourself.

I put myself into a mummy. It was getting cold; it was outside space, where I needed to be. I left the tomb's entrance. Just when I got outside, I could see ashes falling from the sky. Just as quickly, the ashes left when I re-entered the tomb. It was over. Life was trying to tell me to stay with the mummy, because that's where to money is. I stayed and noticed it was getting cold, so I proceeded further underground. I was in the tomb, so I dug. Quicksand. I fell into a sarcophagus. The sand was rotating around, showing passages, mummies and keys, and finally, nothing. I was supposed to be the target. After all, I was in the sarcophagus, and I was the final specimen. The final opening. Everything stopped and restarted to the rotating sand waterfalls.

When I saw an opening, I left for it. Then again everything stopped, spilling onto my starting point and completely covering it. This time, everything opened up a passage, and I took it. The sand was spilling onto me and closed off the entrance to my previous spot, the one I'd just left. When it started spilling onto me I moved, or else I would have been smothered with dust in my lungs and sand in my throat. I could see a flexing face. I was still moving around in a tightly lit sand dune, quicksand, a sarcophagus. I was walking around and saw only a dead end. And if I stopped for real, I saw that flexing face.

The sarcophagus went on and showed dead ends, and back to the tomb I entered. When I saw my body lying there in the tomb, something told me I was not going to like what was going to happen to it. Like watching yourself die in a dream, a nightmare. That and I could not control it; I was just waking up. Here's my premise: if I went back to the mummy and stuffed myself into the body there, bugs would fall out. I left and went back into the sarcophagus. Rotating sand, I remembered the way, and into the sarcophagus.

I took other doors and dropped into the antechamber. When I entered, I saw another mummy. This one was juicy like mine back in the tomb. I thought about why it was there, and upon doing so I wasn't to dig my fingers into the mummy, or bugs would fall out. I needed a way out, and it was clear to me why these juicy mummies were there. People were sleeping, just like me. I re-entered the sarcophagus and saw a mummy there through the rotating sand. This one was not like the others. It was dry, so I entered the chamber this mummy was lying in. I ripped it out of the crypt it was lying in. If I had pushed it in, bugs would fall in.

The mummy's backside had weight packed onto it, and it slowly evaporated in the sarcophagus—quicksand, formaldehyde, crypt, puzzle. These mummies were dry, as if there was a message, a way out, a key. I learned that while asleep in the sarcophagus, I could scare myself awake by the bugs of these rotting corpses, or I could wake up with a clear mind. I did not try the dry mummy; I simply forced myself awake, which led me to a false awakening. I forgot everything and ventured off into my life, never to look back or return home.

I ordered from the store to eat, because I was rich and ate many times. I left the store no longer thinking about hunger. Then I flew away. I flew so high that I fell asleep in my dreams, a second dimension down, a layer. My mind was trained enough because I did not see my body, so I left for some more dreams. And I left for the land, I got scared awake because that mummy had a grip on my life. Everything I remembered in the dreams set my mind up to flex concavely. Upon flexing, the mummy showed me a heavy hallucination in which I was holding a gun. The mummy threw something at me, so it was positive that I was holding a gun, because I really had one in my hand while sleeping. I was intimidated, but I had a gun.

I shot in the right direction and missed one who threw something at me because I thought it was someone else, not the mummy. The force exerted by the shot woke me up and peeled the mummy open. Then I automatically shot into the rotting corpse I was in, and it blew open the right way. That body was toast, and I did not want to be in that frame anymore because bacteria would see me, frightening me to death until I ate myself. I was past the conundrum of how to survive; I would no longer freeze in space.

This muscle I had was permanently flexed, leading my mind to a constructive universe. It led me to a portion peeled away from my body by suction. I was losing air out of my orifices. Because space was sucking my body, this suction flushed something and darted me back into sleep; in my mind, I slept. When I slept, I was shown back to my body up in space somewhere. It showed that a power cell was harvested from the suction power of my body encased in this mummy. It was real the jet pack, but I wasn't. I was microscopic, and the jet pack was idle but on a picture made from this mummy.

Space sucking in, it was wireless. There were a picture there because I was once in there. It was wireless because it was like a picture. If you saw this picture in your mind, you'd know it was operable. Then I was hurled into space from the wireless connection. The matter from the jet pack deemed me small enough to use the jet pack by my wireless connection. Enough matter was shot into the air for the computer of the jet pack to read me—a small, little bacteria. After I continued my habits, I would think, and then see if things were real.

"Oof!" I could see that something had changed. I was still bacterial, but I was with something extra. My mind had a function with this jet pack and was activated wirelessly by the mind. When I left the sucking carcass, I activated the jet pack's computer indefinitely. It hooked onto my body. Although small, the computer was strong enough to propel a little bacteria like me. I took the jet pack all the way out to space to see myself.

Frozen in time, I saw my corpse. I activated my wireless jet pack by climbing into the exoskeleton, the remains of my body, and I was microscopic compared to the jet pack. If I tried, I would be blasted away. I was a piece of bacteria attached to this wireless jet pack signal, out in space. I detached from my wireless jet pack as a piece of bacteria to get into the frozen body. If I attached to the jet pack, I wasn't big enough to operate it, and I would drift away. So I attached myself to my frozen body, which sucked into a power cell. If I attached to the microorganisms, I would be eaten alive, so I attached myself to the frozen part of the body and burrowed deep in the mummy. I was to find the part of the frozen body that was alive, not the bacteria.

I found my way into the mummy. I took my bacterial self to the living part of the carcass just after the bones … the mummy. I understood that the jet pack was real, so I hooked myself just inside the mummy, the frozen mummy. The living part of the carcass, the mummy, I burrowed in there, in the frozen part of flesh. I as bacteria still had a connection to the jet pack because of a wireless connection I had made in the beginning that activated the jet pack indefinitely.

The mummy I shot flushed and made a power cell out in space. I hid the jet pack wireless from my mind, and the muscles of the frozen mummy flexed from the motion of the wireless connection to the jet pack. I as bacteria had rights to an exoskeleton. This exoskeleton I had was my frozen body. When I flexed my frozen body, it put me into stasis, because the muscle relaxed me from the mummy conundrum. Upon doing so, I started hallucinating, but that was okay because it was only a dream about operating the jet pack somewhere in the universe. I unhooked myself to see how I was connected. I was a piece of bacteria hooked into a frozen body as an exoskeleton that was hooked to a jet pack from a rotting body in space. This frozen body had a mummy attached to it and served as an exoskeleton big enough to operate a jet pack out in space. With the ignition of the jet pack, and my body large enough to use the real jet pack, I went out to see this jet pack.

I was finished freezing and went out to check on the star. It was still out in space as beautiful as ever, but it was cold. I had my exoskeleton on, and I was packed with my jet pack. I had my guns that I took with me. I took my jet pack for a ride to see just how cold it was out there. Without my exoskeleton I would freeze, so I shot into the black ahead of the sun. The sun was as hot as ever, and the bullets would not a do a thing to the sun except fall forever; at these distances, they'd fall. So I shot into the black until there was an explosion; this explosion was close … close enough to light up the barrel as the capsule finishes exploding, the bullet outward.

The vastness of space, and the extreme temperatures of it, would create radiation. Radiation was right over there, in space. If I had shot after that explosion, I would have detonated. I found out that space doubles back, but only with something explosive enough to detonate. If you took yourself apart, you would see all the molecules and atoms stretch around for quite some time. A shot of your mind would show unravelled you would be. Into nothing, but atoms everywhere. Just like the atoms your mother carried into you. Nothing. If you saw yourself, you technically doubled back and looked down to see your body, and you brought yourself there from the past. You'd have a look of yourself in the past, two yous.

Due to the radiation, I only had a limited time to do something, so I took myself into stasis to see what that looks like. There would be radiation whizzing at me, and at that level of microscopy, smaller than my body, you would see light there. But in reality, just this cold melted down part of space into what exists rather than light. You could see light in stasis, and radiation in reality. I decided to shoot the radiation into holy smithereens to create a plethora of explosions leading back to the sun until it exploded into either a black hole or it left a nebula.

It was too cold to stay with that sun, because I needed a place for my jet pack. Upon doing that, I realized that the sun did not have enough atoms to grow. I was looking for land. With my mind, I realized there are imprints everywhere, just as there were imprints leading from my past to here. I used my exoskeleton and pulled my head out of stasis from within the muscles that kept me sleeping. When I did, I saw what held me. The star I blew up turned into a nebula, and there was plenty of radiation there, enough light in this stellar neighbourhood.

I went back to the land I came from before I went into stasis. I realized that the land was different than being in stasis, all the way out to the edge of the universe. I had limited time to figure out where to go. I wanted to go back to the other side of space and time. Disconnected, I left my exoskeleton hooked up to the jet pack. I had a wireless connection to the jet pack's computer. Upon getting back outside of my exoskeleton as a baby bacteria, I launched myself into this nebula that I blew up, just over there. It was nice in the clouds because there was heat everywhere. I thought about the jet pack and wondered if the bacteria could hear me. I listened to my mind, and I could say anything. I wondered if there was a such thing as telepathy.

I found a solution. I launched myself back to the jet pack and my exoskeleton. I climbed into the head of the exoskeleton this time because of how it decayed in space. I gently tapped the corpse of the exoskeleton. And nothing. I then took the jet pack exoskeleton for one last ride. I hallucinated that I was operating the jet pack without hurting myself. I propelled the jet pack and asked if the exoskeleton could hear me. It responded and said yes. I knew why he initially did not respond: it was because the rest of the body was just bacteria. There was no intelligent function there, only the exoskeleton responding.

I then asked if he could see me as a baby bacteria, and he said no. But three minutes from now it would respond to the muscles of the exoskeleton after I was out because he could see the movements of the jet pack. I got out of the exoskeleton and launched myself back to the edge of time. I waited for my body to catch up with me, the exoskeleton backpack jet pack. Upon doing so, I used the exoskeleton to launch me back into space. I went on to launch into space as a baby bacteria. When I left the exoskeleton backpack jet pack, I launched myself over there, away from the true location of the exoskeleton. The further I went into space, I saw the real meaning of the backpack jet pack.

When I was over there, not farther than the limits of space, I launched myself farther into space. Nothing. Then I launched some more. I came into view of the backpack jet pack after I launched myself once more. I thought about why I was farther from the exoskeleton than from the backpack jet pack. I thought about it some more and realized that the backpack jet pack was farther than it seemed because I am just a baby bacteria. In view of the backpack jet pack, I jumped one last time by the CPU's command to the jet pack. A baby bacteria hook into the backpack jet pack, or hook myself into the exoskeleton bacteria? I didn't want to bother my jet pack with a baby bacteria.

I thought about it, and I hooked myself into the exoskeleton bacteria and made my way to the mummy of the backpack jet pack. I was with the backpack jet pack and took it for a spin. I launched myself into the mouth of the bacteria. I thought, *If I launch myself into the muscle, I will hit it.* So I burrowed myself deep in the flesh of the dead part of the exoskeleton, the part that fused. I knew where I was in reality. When I saw the exoskeleton flex dead tissue, I relaxed. When I launched myself surrounded by dead tissue, the backpack had me pushing into the dead tissue because it launched you, the bacteria. This bothered the exoskeleton enough that it turned around and adjusted the backpack jet pack onto the back of the exoskeleton.

I was uncomfortable in the exoskeleton, so I jetted myself into the webbings of the exoskeleton. This was simply me jumping into the flesh of the exoskeleton to relax my muscles. When I relaxed myself, I operated the jet pack while flexing the mummy's muscles. I got out because that was it. I burrow myself in the supposedly dead flesh to operate the jet pack. This flesh wasn't dead; the mummy could feel it. I found out what was at the other side of space: a jet pack and an exoskeleton.

It was true that I was small enough to be propelled by it, this anti matter, this jet pack. Because when this jet pack was primed, it inherited my DNA to act as the being inside of the jet pack, a sensor that only responded to the sensitivity of the touch of the being it came from. The jet pack also served as a picture with wireless communication to anyone who could see it and was small enough to have the potential to fly, like being bacterial. I would not have skin touching my mind unless I became sick. Only money should touch me and this robot.

If I had done it the other way, I would have killed someone I loved. Just some random guy with a hat, your friend. He would have fallen, and his hat would have fallen off his head to hit the floor with him. If I had done this any other way, I would have been told to wake up for sure. But having been awakened, I would have jumped awake the wrong way and would have ripped the mummy the right way, and you would have died bleeding to death, rigor mortis, from pulling the wrong muscle. You needed the concentration of the dreams with the mummy, or else you would have ruined yourself. Indeed, shot yourself.

I wanted to know what was at the other side of these cryptic passages. When I woke up right, my mind fell asleep next to my robot. I was with my mind before, but that fell asleep and was no longer with the robot in my mind. Everything that I thought about before falling asleep was now real, so I had to leave and I did not see any of the robot's people. In fact, I could not look at myself anymore, because I was not that guy. I am who I thought I was. I left, and I was in a society earlier than mistakes. I was ahead of crime, boastfulness.

When we collected supplies from the remaining land, we lit a fire with the supplies and created signals of smoke. We made sure that all the land could see us. If the people of the oceans couldn't make contact, they made contact with the people of the land and further inland to the other side of the land at that ocean. In a community not far from people's houses, people were shopping in stores in peace until the Big Bang hit, before the Big Bang. These stores were all imaginary because the Big Bang and the quantum universe deemed it so, because they didn't exist.

It went like this: In the beginning, there was nothing, such that there was so much peace that we slept until thirteen billion years later. For thirteen billion years, your ancestors were bouncing around until you were born. In the beginning there were shopping, bills paid, mortgages funded, vehicles fixed, and streets paved. Everybody had Nobel prizes and doctorate degrees. There were no diseases, as everything was cured. When there was a cure for nothing, they took it apart for the cure, the vaccination, for this disease that was supposed to not exist. When they had the disease contained, they vaccinated it and then cured it so that it didn't exist.

When nuclear winter hit, everything was gone from the shelves quicker than my Molotov cocktail. I was supposed to use it for the games. It would be treason to throw the Molotov over during nuclear winter because, like the beginning, people everywhere knew what peace looked like. And like the beginning, they threw the Molotov over for games, which is a part of peace because they were just games. Because of nuclear winter, I threw the bottle over my head, and it ignited. Just like the games, I would do it where everyone would be able to see it. Because of the Big Bang, everything only had moments of peace because these peaceful acts were not done all at once. And when I threw the cocktail over my head, it was like peace because it was like the games' signal, thrown over a building, to signify the games.

You had only moments of peace at a time because all the remaining symbols of peace were gone with the Big Bang, or they had not happened yet. You needed to make peace again or face a future that was not supposed to be right—always on your feet, working in a psychiatric centre or in jail, if you resisted. I had to leave because people who had seen me were getting suspicious that I threw the bottle and would not leave. When I left, they would be notified about fallout. They would notice and copy peace because whenever peace struck, we were all notified by its beauty. Whenever you saw peace, it would light up the land with its beauty.

Stories were starting to pop up because of the Big Bang, Molotov cocktails, or pieces of the games. Moments of peace in the games were seen by the Molotov cocktail being thrown, but not full peace. They threw one over in the name of peace or not. We had to either participate in games during nuclear winter, which was like walking out to be intentionally harmed, or take it as a sign of peace to see if there really was a nuclear winter. We would have to go house to house, village to village, town to town, city to city, planet to planet, or solar system to solar system, even galaxy to galaxy, black hole to black hole, and virtual reality to virtual reality, to catch any sign of what that nuclear winter would be.

We would catch the criminals copying nuclear winter and see if anybody was born in nuclear winter, at the host of many like a hive of sociopaths and to see if there were any survivors. And like the beginning, people gathered to see the cocktail, or people like me, with knowledge of peace, were starting to become aware for other things to happen. If you didn't do it the right way, you would lose concentration.

People like me were the first to happen because you would do things the way you did. After the Big Bang, there was no peace because people had to make it. Time and time again you would make something and then it would be used up until it made fossil fuels, like using up the item into dirt, then nothing.

If I became fully aware, we would see what would happen if I threw the cocktail, and no one would notice it and no one would come. That was the worst part, but then it occurred to me that it must have happened before, but not necessarily by me, because I was then thinking about it. I had to change something … it was just a matter of what. Things that had happened were about to change and not necessarily had changed. Things that have happened did not change a thing, or else I would have noticed it.

During the beginning, I made one Molotov cocktail out of a bottle, some fuel, and a cloth.

I filled the bottle up with fuel and stuffed a cloth in the mouth of the bottle. Molotov cocktail. All I needed was a lighter of some kind to light up the cloth and to break the Molotov cocktail for ignition, spreading the flame in a wild fire. I needed a Molotov cocktail because we used them in games and for practice. The initial flag says throw a Molotov cocktail over, or a Molotov cocktail was thrown over your head, in the likes of fallout. Molotov cocktail.

There was a Molotov cocktail sitting there. I picked it up. There were rations. I made food in advance of the camp. I made a Molotov cocktail for fallout and threw it over my head. While eating, I biked up the block and saw nothing. I was riding my bike, a flag bike with three wheels that let me sit in it face-down like the ones used in competitions, in tournaments. It had a hand crank and stands up when I take off like a unicycle. This bike was made for the Olympics. "For the Olympics." I took out my Molotov cocktail. "Molotov cocktail."

I saw nothing. Because nothing was in use. There was something there. Molotov cocktail. The street games were on; everybody with a bike made for injuries were welcome to participate with sports equipment. The games began because I went down to get my bike, and some people took off past me. A joke and a way of life. See someone bike by you while they see your sweet bike starting up the games. My bike.

They were doing nothing. "Doing nothing." Molotov cocktail. I threw one over. I made one earlier. A Molotov cocktail.

"I, could see from the street; the street was imagining things, like me walking on it. The street welcomed me in. I imagined the street leaned in to hug me." I wandered up the block. I went to get my picnic behind a grassy cover bush clearing where I stashed my goods. I was only allowed to get it in third person view, because that's where the picnic was—in third person view, over your head. Like being in a secret passage made just for you. They were doing something. I saw with my eyes closed, because I thought about it. I saw because it was easy. I saw.

There was a destructive mess. I wandered up the street, up the street. "I saw. And it was." I talked about it in detail. They saw my bike. I biked up the street and saw nothing. I talked about it in detail because I had my eyes closed. Closing my eyes while talking was easy. My head darted silently, and I was peeking. You could see a man's face peeking. I biked up the block and saw everything, crime. I biked up the block. I came home safely. They were stretched out in the middle of a damaging act.

"Everybody out!" The police cleaned up the scene after me. I was thinking about people wandering around real fast, like watching an ET or shadow person to and from their location as fast as you can think, but not faster. An old woman sewing. Piles of rocks. They were wandering around because they could see. They could see others, so they followed, careful to be inconspicuous from following others' actions. Dance. Speculate. They could see people. "They made up the word," thoughts, sounds, and dead people. With their bare-naked, eyes, they saw thoughts, sounds, and dead people. Blindness. Eyes closed. They were thinking about dead people, the ones they saw. They saw. Dead people were all connected to the mind, thoughts, and the past. "Past." Blindness.

They were bound to walk around forever in thought since they no longer had bodies, in the past. Past. They came over. Gone forever, a toast to burning up the pasts, fuels, the sun. So much so that the shape of the planet was changed to the weight of the past. Inconspicuous. Time travel. They saw how to live, and it was just a matter of who would get to that technological advancement first. "Of course, they would roam the planet in search of their bodies, their skeletons, to meet their maker."

Maker. Blindness. It was Halloween. It was like them wandering aimlessly and then peeking into their minds, watching themselves.

They wandered around aimlessly. I changed my clothes. They walked to the event horizon. They walked to the limits of their imagination. They tested the waters by trying it out to see if their thoughts were true according to reality. According to reality. "Reality." You could see a boy lean over to tell a girl something. War. Like walking to a UFO and leaving forever in space. You could see the body, the back of the person watching inside of the black hole. Glowing eyes. You could see a boy lean over and tell a girl something. War. Waiting to leave. Waiting to leave. A girl asks a boy something. "Forever." Forever. The, back of a person. They saw. They saw something cheap.

There was a construction site immediately in front of me, like everything picked up and crawled on their knees to this site. On their knees crawling because, suddenly, everything was. They asked me a secret. They told me a secret. "When they told me, I understood." Understood. Like being immediately in front of me while being in a car, showing up to a construction site, they are, immediately, in front of me. "They told. They told." They asked me a secret. "They were up to something in front of me. Told me." And then they were working at the same time. So how could they see the future?

"They set everything up. Set everything up" and tore it down. They tore it down and anticipated people's thoughts by seeing what you would think while standing there before anyone else does. They were saying if they were there, they were either thinking about the set or what they were doing. Doing, like they wanted in the set, like they wanted in the set, or to just, or to just, stand there. They were thinking. Thinking. If they were doing something, then I'd know so, and furthermore, I'd know what to do with the set if they were doing something to it. Doing something to it.

I saw this girl. I checked to see if they needed it. I saw this girl and she was texting. I'd know if they did something. Texting about being psychic, about how psychoanalysis works, about how someone said something and how it pertained to you in your mind as what you would do in that situation, or would have done compared to them. Because I left and came back when I thought about something, I thought that I must be doing something or else I would be thinking about doing something. If they were standing there thinking about the set, I'd know. If they were thinking about the set while standing there and started playing with their minds about the set, I'd be weary to take command. If they just stood there, they had an insulting thought, I thought, or else they were mad that they could not enter the set and then cursed the world. I'd know.

I was thinking that if I stood there in that spot, I could see what they thought. I moved there after a while when this girl left. She was thinking about texting. I thought that this girl must have thought about the set while standing there. And she thought *That sucks. I could not enter the set.* I asked a lot of questions. They peered in the door. If they could be in a relaxed state enough to see their minds, you could hear them chanting to get what they wanted, and all thoughts leading to just what everyone really was up to and thinking.

There was a crowd there, people in peace. I saw the truth. They were hiding something from me. "Hiding." Hiding. But that wasn't necessarily the case, because I was only thinking that they were hiding something. I wandered up the block. From me, I thought. A fight. Wander up the block. I saw so many people, their faces, and to me it was like they were all frozen in time because I could recall what they looked like in my mind. My dreams. I woke up. To some, that's a far cry. People lurking, like piles of meat. The meat self picking up when they wanted to leave, like a wobbling fish who washed ashore standing up and walking on the sand. They were picking up animals. They were not animals but behaved like that, the wobbling meat.

Return. I. "Running." Running. Running from war. "War! So many I saw, I thought about." My first instinct was to duck and hide, and peek when I saw them. When I saw them, I peeked. I would have looked weird in the middle of nowhere, alone, a cold breeze on my left shoulder, like walking around at night. Shoulder. My shoulder, the breeze hugged me. If it wasn't my shoulder, that would be like my friend walking up to a stranger and hugging him or her. The breeze on your shoulder. They would hug them for a show, or there was something wrong, if there was something wrong, awfully wrong. Walk up to a stranger's house and become their friend, like the new kid on the block. Molotov cocktail. A ghost's rigor mortis decaying hand grabbing your shoulder, flexing nerves. They felt friendly, and just as quickly would decay if it looked too suspicious. I was imagining things.

"I started up the car. I imagined being in a room full of people while being invisible. Their minds looked like they might crawl out to notice me because the mind is known to see truth or speculation, spiritual in nature, mundane, mystical, or psychic. That or my own mind would notice, which would be twice as mysterious because I could do it myself. I peeked into my mind; you could see a face in the corner of your eye." To others, their thoughts might have been out of shape. To see someone, at first thought, you would need to have learned something to make you think from solid judgement. Then you could dart your head in recognition of seeing a crowd of people while looking at them or seeing something, theoretically. You saw.

I thought rapid thoughts while on the way there to this crowd of people. My mind raced. I stopped to sit down while looking at them for a while to spy on them. I peeked. I peeked into my mind to start thinking all that I could think. Decay. Decaying body. This was to let their thoughts settle that they saw me, like kids walking around in your mind and slapping the tummy and head of a dead body, just in recognition that you could think at all. I really didn't dart my head in recognition of seeing these people. I darted my head in recognition that I had seen these people afterwards in my mind. I saw. I darted my head silently inside my mind, in my mind in recognition of these people I saw in front of me. I darted. After a while, I felt paranoid. I was sitting there because I was sitting there. I did not want to be noticed by these people for sitting for too long; that's when I really darted my head around in my mind. "Was I seen?" Seen. "Were they spying on me?"

I saw. I was watching them, darting my head continuously in my mind. Seen, I'm glad I wasn't. Like imagining a story. "Him, that was him." Was that him? The man whom I saw in my mind? I focused on my head in my mind. I gave up. I got up, continued my journey onward to this crowd. "Onward this crowd." I hid to spy on them, because I did not know what to think from up the block. Molotov cocktail. I was in the middle of a performance. I was the same as them, expecting me—a complete stranger—as they were to me working up the block. Molotov cocktail. I threw it. "Threw it." I spied on them from moments away in time. Moments away in time. Molotov cocktail going over. When I sat down on the street, that's when I really started spying on them, but they didn't know ... just that I was a random man sitting there, if they noticed me.

Not while I was on my way to sit down, but when I sat, I really noticed them. I noticed them, and then I started to feel paranoid. That's when I darted my head in my mind. "Everybody out." It was my finale to get up from being seen for sitting too long and to be seen just right by the crowd if they looked. "Looked." In light, I saw the night. They were spying on me. They were spying on me, up the street, I could see. In a mystical mind, I could see. And I was spying because they had not noticed me yet, from moments away. Doctor Pathic. I felt as though from up the street things were going in slow motion. Motion.

"Like they were watching TV and ignoring real life. To turn away from what was real and, like being asleep, so much time going by." Going by. "Like being further away, slowed down in time."

It happens only a split second at a time, every time. Ripples in the universe through time. Molotov cocktail. And not every time is the same, because you either thought at the time and your thoughts changed the way you think, or you moved something and that changed the way you act. Molotov cocktail. One going over. I saw them, working, because that's what it looked like. Working. Molotov cocktail. If they hadn't noticed me, "A cocktail going over," it was as though they were sneaking around in their minds. I waved my hand just once to see if their peripherals were working, and they were concentrating. Sneaking around in their minds.

The way reality is built is like everybody works, even when you don't intend to, because you take care of yourself, moving things for yourself. If not for yourself, then for someone else you work for. Molotov cocktail. You moved things and heard about them later from jobs around the city or town, country, or even the world. Like your stuff is famous. Molotov cocktail. It is like a ghost moving things around and finally coming to see you after you've left, after you've moved things that were your business. Molotov cocktail. Like while up the street, downtown, and through another block in a different reality. Someone had moved things for you. Someone moved things for you in their reality and while dormant. The things you moved were of another reality in their reality. And by praising, things moved by others are another reality, unless you think you can live what they have in the same reality, take their place, pick up their stuff in your job that was once theirs that you now consume. That is called another reality because you are then doing something someone was doing, and with all their credentials. You are definitely living another reality that is now your own.

It seems jobs come from multiple places of reality. Like when you worked for yourself, the thing you moved was correspondent to your mind, another time waiting for that old robot to pass while you were still up the street, downtown, and through another block in a different reality, just like the one you thought about. You picked up their stuff to live their reality. Like a meta subliminal reality, a training ground set in space somewhere where the ground was hard enough to stand on while still in space with no light from the stars. A quad liminal reality while in space, where I would not fall either, due to gravitation. The beginning to my reality, then to start fraud. Gravitation. Like a graviton, holding me up like the sun holds up.

I didn't want to fall. I wanted to relax. Relax. I didn't want my feet up to relax: the connotation of relax, the silly old joke where it's your turn to do something, and the others relax with their feet up in the air with a big old sigh. I just wanted to lie down and relax. That's how these people made me feel working in front of me. I felt worried, thinking about relaxing. Like work continued while you were home. You feel worried that you missed work. Feel worried you missed work. I felt safe, because I just showed up. "Just, showed up." Not uneased by the new sights. I was safe, so I could think how I wanted. Do how I wanted. I was feeling safe. But I was a paranoid. I wasn't being hurt while these people were in front of me doing something, because they were working. "Safety." Metaphysically, it was possible to be hurt in my feelings, but only if you were there metaphysically, like say in another reality, up the block, up the street, downtown, and in another reality copying my thoughts.

I was safe. I felt like I was safe. I felt that way because there was no one threatening me. "And the only things connecting reality were a similar spot just up the street; from another block they were thinking while you were on that spot. A similar thought, the same as you. And you could see in your mind them working. And on that thought, when they worked, you thought about the deeds they were doing with the street and tested it to see if the work was right. You tested it by seeing if the thought corresponded to the working street in reality. They were on the same block; no one was being hurt, and again someone might have been hurt by, say, daydreams, hallucinations, or drugs. It would be like being on another block, up the street, downtown, and in another reality near a black hole or near a place where the shape of it was exactly they way it happened for you.

Reality. The reality is that they could have been hurt if at the same time you thought about a thought, and another thought the same thought you were thinking while they were on drugs or sleeping, dreaming of being on another block, up the street, downtown, and in another reality. "Another reality." They were up the block in another reality. Until I realized what was going on. "Going on." Again, I was paranoid. At my house is where I left my life, and I would not know what to do if I arrived first at my house when this was going on all the way up to my house. Could I have been ambushed? Might I have been followed? Who were they? They were doing something constructive and fun, so I decided to watch them, just in case something happened that I could participate in. I was happy because it looked like the public was welcome. Public was welcome. I didn't know why, though.

While I was at a distance from them, I watched them, but I was still paranoid. I started doing what they were doing, and I noticed something funny. They were moving things out of the UFO. A man was smiling and then stopped smiling. I wondered why. "I continued my job and noticed that they were abducting people." Abducting people. "I could not make out why, so I continued to abduct the people there too." There too. And I didn't know the public was welcome. "Welcome."

There was a strange craft there, noiseless. I did not want to stop because it looked like these people were doing the right thing, and if so, not the correct thing. "Correct thing. Everything was down." Everything was down with it. The streets were all working with lights on, but from the corner of my eye I noticed a man standing and looking at me. He was wearing a construction helmet and an orange safety vest. He was looking right at me. Just staring. He stared at me, hard, and when I gave up and turned away, I looked back and he was gone in under two seconds. I noticed and started thinking about death, and if I would die or not. A daydream, and I daydreamt that I was getting hacked up like someone rushing up the block to get me. I could see shadows cast onto a building right in front of me, and someone being hacked up. I couldn't believe it. Someone could tell what I was thinking? It was dark and only the background of the shadow was lit up on the wall.

I started to walk across the ground to see the peculiarity of my mind, if someone was hacked up. Suddenly, the lights flashed on and there was animatronic robot standing there. The scene of being hacked up was gone within the shadow. When I started thinking again, the animatronic bot started toward me and took off left to his right, my left. He frightened me. Then the lights turned off again and the robot was gone. I could only see the outline of the shadow of this would-be robot. I could see the shadow of these robots frozen, and nothing happened. When I started my daydream again, I got used to these robots scaring me. This time I thought about getting the hell out of there, in my daydream, because that scared me. Then I could see the shadows shuffling, like they were walking away, and they were gone.

I was thinking about leaving. I knew they were copying me, but I didn't know how. That scared me again. I was just about ready to leave when the lights flashed on, the panels closed off a certain way, and the shadows were gone. I walked away. As I walked away I noticed that there were even more dolls this time; through an entrance I walked, and they were on. This time, they were slowly moving, like a ride, playing something, then someone laughed real loud. That scared me. When they were done, the lights turned off and I could hear laughing, like scaring someone was funny. That frightened me. I decided to take a walk through the black to see what was up with those dolls. I was curious to find out.

When I walked into the black, the lights turned off behind me. It was dark, and when I least expected walking forwards again, those dolls turned on in front of me. That scared me. Without wasting any time, I saw that they were waving, like they knew I was there. I was still curious. I was there and nothing; only when I walked into the dark did they turn on. I heard loud shouts coming from nowhere, nowhere I could see these dolls talking the same as acting. The man shouting sounded like an old man who was scared to death, ready to yell at someone to scare them while he was scared, a war cry, scared, like a fight. Scared me. Like my being reconciled that I was there, and I felt they turned on by my commitment.

I walked further into the dark and heard another man yelling that scared me, coming from the dark, and the signs turned on for me again. This time they were showing that they were waving bye and were off somewhere. I walked further into the dark and this time no machines turned on, except lights went off and showed a man pointing. When I went that way it showed a robot laughing, and lights were then on me. When I left further into the black, it showed someone crying, and I was laughing silently in my head.

Then I proceeded to leave and the animatronics turned off and showed the way out. I left and another set of bots turned on. I went that way and it scared me. When I left and the lights turned off behind me, I turned around quickly and walked back in. Upon doing so, I heard screaming from the black. A sensor went off, with no light this time. A male screaming. The same dolls waving bye were on. I went to check on these dolls, to get a closer look, and a light flashed on, showing a man and a sign. I backed up and went back into the dark; lights turned on me and you could hear a man talking. After the man quit talking, everything turned off, and again I could see some signs being covered by an apparition, picturing a light turned off showing a sign behind the black, a shadow. There it showed a man juggling as a shadow cast onto the wall, forever. The juggling didn't stop, it just went on.

Another sign lit up. I looked at it and heard laughing from behind me, in the direction the man juggling. A man juggling. Laughing. It didn't stop. I left that scene, and this time, while walking through the dark, the lights flicked on, the exit. I left to exit, on toward the exit lights. When I reached the lights, the lights never turned off. On the lights were. It looked like an exit. At the cusp of leaving, I had to push the exit sign. A man pointed out the way, the way to go. Upon doing so, something jumped out on top of me. That scared me.

I left into the light, and this time a light to my right, then another light, turned on, and a clown scared me who jumped out instantaneously from behind a sign. The clown backed up into the dark behind him. Then a light turned on, followed by, "You'll never eat me alive!" I walked through the exit. And I hit dead end. To my left there was another sign. I walked over to it, touched it. Then, nothing. I freaked out a little and turned around. Nothing. I was ready to squat and cry, but my attention turned behind me. I went over there because a giant "eat me alive" sign was gone. A fun house. I walked in there because there was a way. Then upon entering the way, the lights turned on and panels flipped down. One where a clown walked up to stand on, and another showing an illusion, a hallway.

I walked into the hall and heard loud steppin' shoes, steppin' loud behind me, running up to me. The clown followed me in; I got scared. I walked further into the hall and was engulfed by blow up balloons. I entered the balloons onward. I walked into the dark of the maze balloons and reached a dead end with a scary face painted on it, showing teeth. I walked back through the balloons to the exit, hopefully, and I was abducted. I went into the maze after a quick second, a rest, it felt like I had. The signs were on, and this time talking. I sighed. Thank god I was only in a maze.

I left and saw the exit sign—a hand pointing. Upon trying to make my exit, a hand came from nowhere and smeared my face, like smell. I turned away and nothing. When I turned away, I left into a dark spot, and I saw a living being jumping around who scared the life out of me. I turned around, and another light was on a sign. I left to it, and I saw a man go to the bathroom. He said, "Heyoujubgubo." I left. I did not want to do that again.

I ventured forward, and there was another sign. A girl holding a teddy bear. I did not want to enter there again because there was a sign up, just like the others. Then I walked into the dark of the maze, and a light turned on. There was a man digging in the garbage. I guess that was a step up from just holding garbage. Before I went, the man held up garbage and looked at me, and the lights turned off. I heard something drop, and then the clown who dug in the garbage scared the life out of me in his steppin' shoes. And that was it. I was sad, and went to sleep.

Upon sleeping, I kept seeing people left, right, and centre. Only people. And then I saw a sign; it was either a far cry with the people or enter the sign way. I entered the sign and I saw people everywhere, much like the steppin' shoe clown, who scared me. I looked at the sign and entered the sign. People were looking in all directions. The maze looked exactly like the one before. I was sure I'd been abducted. I realized what was going, then I woke up.

When I woke up, I thought about my dreams and everything that had happened so far: signs, people, dreams. I thought hard about my dream and realized I'd seen those people before. They were real people, and the last person, a sign, was a clown, the one who picked up garbage and scared me. Where there was a clown, where I saw this garbage bag clown, there was a sign in my dreams, and it was exactly proportionate to the garbage bag, steppin' shoe clown. I realized that others with signs while awake were exactly like me. I woke up, after concentrating.

I went to this steppin' shoe clown and started a riot. I scared him left, right, and centre. Hours went by. I caught up to him and scared him again. I decided to try something. I decided to scare the living hell out of him. He stopped, and I ran up to him, then I scared him with a sign. Then I left everything on, and a moment went by. He then took a look around.

The signs turned on and off, as you would see them regularly, on and off. When it turned off, he noticed a clown making him jump starting my way, and noticed the signs one last time, from his peripherals. The light went on, then off, and then I ran up to him, flashing lights, a sign on, more clutter from behind him because I threw something. Finally, the lights went off. I picked him up in reality then I drove from my UFO because I couldn't see and I wanted to scare him from the g's of gravity.

I went out to space and then turned on the body massager. I crawled into stasis, my body dissolved, and I took him faster. I left the UFO running. I left everything on and let him get so sacred that he ran into a corner. Little did he know that the corners of the ship were built for combat or self defence. When the AI asked him what he wanted, he told and took everything with him, scared to death. I changed back into my other, the one where signs don't come alive.

The construction man's light was on and it didn't turn off. It was clearly to creep me out, and this clown had a sign just over there. I went to it. After a while the light turned off, and this time I saw what the construction would do with the lights off. He slowly peeked, walking backwards, riding backwards, disappearing behind a wall, a silhouette, a shadow. Then nothing. I walked out to see nothing. And lights on me. They were forever. I stayed in the light. I saw another inviting sign, I wanted to see if the sign did anything. It just showed a smiling man and didn't turn off. It didn't turn off. I could wait until the power was out, but that was just too long. I was curious about what the sign would do to the opposite side of the way things seem.

When I walked into the dark, I didn't want to be in anyone's way, so I ditched into the light on the other side of the sign. Upon arriving, another sign turned on, showing a man smiling. I walked into the dark, and all the lights turned off. Then I quickly turned around back in the black, after the lights turned off. Then, surprise! Screaming, and that clown abducted me.

In the beginning, there were nothing but signs and life leading all the way back from your ancestors, then Jesus, then dinosaurs, then extremophiles, and rats in your family, all the way back to your great ancestry into the beginning. Then other rats and cute bugs all leading back to the fact that they once existed, in the beginning. And this is where you came from.

Atoms have a half life so that they would once decay. And molecules have a half life of when they decay also, but the point is that you could maintain molecules and when that time is done, they could change completely. In the beginning just after the Big Bang, there was nothing but space and radiation. Then the Big Bang. You need to work out your muscles and keep doing that so you change kinetically. This means that you change all the molecules in your body to make a body for yourself, so that you can live in space. Molecules transform from simple atoms to ions, then back into nutrients for the body. Do this change from molecules, and you could completely.

After the Big Bang, the being wanted to step out into space. He needed space, and that's what the Big Bang offered.

Radiation

Mummy

Crypt

Mummy

Radiation

Mummy

Tomb

Mummy

Space

The being used the mummy to blind him and give rise to hallucinations within. He was instructed to leave hallucinations alone and make an extra body. So he let the mummy rot some more and flexed those muscles again. And when the mummy rotted out some more, he flexed his muscles. He flexed his muscles hard enough so that the bone came alive.

You dragged that ragged body of yours into the light, and you made yourself hallucinate. This was to prevent you from the feeling of burning to death when you worked on the power cell, all the while preserving you so that your mind worked. You ripped your mind out of concentration, preventing you from seeing something else, even if you were thinking in your mind. You wanted to be free. When your mind was strong enough, by learning, you crawled out of there. You ripped your body out of concentration. During your journeys hallucinating, you thought about many people in class, until you concentrated.

You did not want to see people in your mind. During your time hallucinating, you etched many designs onto the brain of the mummy so that you could think. You etched designs onto your body by hallucinating so you would not feel the feeling of burning to death while working on the power cell. Back in the day. Then you cast this organ into the fire and threw the tomb in as well. And you walked into it to stomp on the land filled with fire, to rescue gold, and you threw the gold in to use liquid magma to melt it some more. Upon doing so, you walked further into the fire and stomped more gold out, and you fused it into more.

You did this until the star cooled enough so that when it cooled it was far enough to light up the land. The fire was only lit up, but not at fusion. So you dug your hand into the star to rip out the radiation. You waxed and waned the innards of the star until was hot enough to fuse and light up space. It seems that when it was hot enough, the fire from space was fused all around, making the density of a sun from space cool at equilibrium, creating the illusion of a floating sun. And you fell out of the sky as the sun receded into the distance, like it was showing goodbye. But what really happened is that the sun fell into orbit; it flew away to abide by the rules of gravity, and your body then proceeded to fall into orbit too, orbit of the star. All that was left was a star, and space.

It was getting cold, so you hiked up the block in space where there was enough gravity to create pits in space time, like a water well, rotating and ready to dissipate. Space was there to walk on. It was getting cold.

I was awarded the land and a tomb.

I noticed a picture, and it was of the back of a man's head. There was a man bent over arresting the other that was there. The picture was weird because it showed the back of a man's head. Back of a man's head. The back of the man's head was clear who it was in the picture. Because it looked like the back of a man's head from the picture. Because it was strange the man worked harder and harder, his head in the picture to get the job done was focused, sweating. I watched him because of everything I'd seen. He stopped smiling; he worked harder and harder. I needed to check this man out. I'd seen the picture in the UFO and seen the back of a man's head. I peeked into the UFO to see their fine work.

There was someone on an examining table on screen and not in reality. It looked like a screen at the back side of the room; one was finished being abducted opposite from where I was based. He was in the room but no longer there, like he'd dissolved. He was in the room. I peeked my head in at once but appeared on screen this man. "Peeked my head in." But it looked like they took apart his body by flashing an X-ray on him, rotating his bones and flexing his skin into pure muscle. Pure muscle. They hooked up his mind to the electricity so that they could get him on screen by simply aligning the picture with his body, or else hold him down and align his body with the picture. They flushed his organs to appear on screen and see that it was working, putting his bones at rest in first place. "First place. Bones at rest. Place." Bones at rest. Doctor Pathic. "They saw that everything worked, so they turned on the power to set his bones in the technology the right way." Technology the right way. Technology the right way.

Another light turned on. I checked to see why, and it was so that the bones flushed first. It was set this way so that the bones did not fry him while sedated in stasis while in the UFO and while he didn't fry while being put on screen, to be screened. To be screened. That and when done with it, it would make a deadly laser by frying bones, if we were doing that. "For protection." Upon doing so, I checked the back of the man's head inconspicuously, because the picture was like that. I didn't know why. "I looked around the room of the UFO again." When I looked again, I noticed what the man's face looked like in the UFO, inside the screen, who was once lying on the table. His face was distorted; he had no face, like magic was making his face twist. I was worried about things, and that was not the greatest of my concerns. I saw the hardworking man work even harder when I checked back on him, and it was really weird because of how he was working. "Working." He kept up pace moving things from the UFO outside. I wasn't doing that because I was not like him. Why? Because my determination was great, and I did not have evil deeds in my mind. My work was based on constructiveness. Not taking things out of the UFO while they clearly needed to be put away. I put things away. I would have used the mechanical tools and stuff instead of taking them out. The man working hard was really brainwashed, and the technology within the UFO was showing what his mind looked like. His mind looked like.

During my time, another peeked in the UFO and saw his head, the picture. Upon doing so, I looked at the UFO and noticed that the were moving tools out working really hard. I saw that was right, and when I saw the people in the screen take his picture, it developed the back of his head. I knew that was wrong; we weren't going to like seeing the back of this man's head. So we abducted him. We strapped him to the table and massaged his muscles into pure muscle to take apart his body. We flushed his organs; we turned on the X-ray and then headed to put his bones in the X-ray machine. When that was finished, we saw a light turned on to ensure his bones weren't fried while in stasis and sedated in the X-ray machine. "What's in the X-ray machine?" What's in the X-ray machine? "What's in the X-ray machine?"

They dropped the picture into the machine and we turned to see what that was about. "You could see his face." We needed to position his body right so that we could see what his body looked like while he was being abducted inside the picture, the back of his head. We used mechanical tools like found on a construction site and drilled where we needed. We drilled a hole, right there in the UFO, because that's where he showed up on screen in his mind. They picked him up. To sedate him. Doing what was correct, not right. It was our notion that drilling the right way meant strapping you in the UFO while inside technology. Something told me that we were not going to like seeing the back of this man's head.

"The back of this man's head." It would be like drilling him in real life, but instead of his place on the table, it was where he showed up in the technology. And the spot we drilled, on screen, would show a picture of what his mind looked like. We strapped his mind in by drilling spots on the UFO where his mind was. We took off in a UFO. He was really struggling, keeping parts of his body from being seen on screen because he was really thinking about those parts. We took the deed by being there, and so did I by showing up. We needed to see the back of this man's head, so we did everything in our power to show it while he was on screen and in the UFO.

When we could no longer understand what we were looking at, we flew the craft to clean out the signals coming from the technology by flying there as we saw in the program and operating the switch to get the right projection. If it made no sense, we restrained him. When we found out, we drilled the spot and put everything up. We did not let random holes be drilled with random rivets put in. "Random rivets put in." We rebuilt the craft after every time it was used and after random holes like that were drilled, and after rivets were ripped in and out from projections. We always ripped out the interior and almost always replaced everything; the only thing keeping us from doing it was this final job, so our score was perfect.

When they showed us their evil deeds, we gave them free UFO rides. "Free UFO rides." And when they told us, we let them have freedom. "Freedom." You picked up the drill and tested it by drilling the air, a test run to see where the signal on the screen was, as the drill's power could be seen on screen, traced and tracked, to see where you would drill and see if it worked. "See if it worked." If they drilled what was on screen, the body, they lost a signal. Luckily, they were only on screen when you drilled and missed. To find the signal again, they looked up the signal from the internet and projected it to the screen on board the UFO. Board the UFO. "When they drilled, they were looking for the mind of the man who was abducted that was strapped in." Strapped in.

When they participated and gave up all intel for everything, including the safety of others, they used the UFO. And while in flight, they took the rivet out and let them go and rebuild everything in the name of the UFO and the fantastic work that the former suspect had tied and had ties to. Blackness. They let you see the rivet being taken out, which gave you power. Doing that was easier than seeing the distorted face first and then wrestling him down, but regardless, we needed to see his faceless and distorted face, whether we wrestle him down or whether we tricked him. It had to be done. Our job was to make sure we didn't see the man's distorted face off screen, and the back of his head. "Back of his head. If we seen the back of this man's head after they took his picture, that wouldn't be good because he abducted some one inside his mind. Back of this man's head."

They, the people whom we hated most, not feared. What we really feared was our own program, because we are more constructive than they were. We are advanced, so we knew we were packing the punch. Packing the punch. The program, god help us if it were ever used on us, is what we feared. That and there was nothing there where people were shown to, because they worry you then show you to make you scared, they did. "Scared, they did; they showed you sights. It was just a constructed feeling combined by telling you worrying things and waking you up when not ready; these beings show you to get at you."

In another scenario, they drugged you and dropped you off in the middle of the street, one that matched your mind after they quizzed you. If you didn't come to, you were abducted again. Reverse psychology. It would only seem right if they did the opposite when you were up the street, when their defences were down for them to you. "Reverse psychology." That and if you did the opposite to them by not thinking about up the street, and walking free from on board, where they let you go to a place that messed with your feelings, but you would be safe. When they dropped you off "up the street," a place that they told you a bunch of things about and messed with your feelings about, you would be stranded. You would make gunpowder and blow up something electronic in your mind to distort the image they saw on you if you wanted. This should give you a way out.

Another way out was if they hypnotized you and they dropped you off up the street for real and did something to your mind to make it seem like you were still on board the craft, just walking away. If you couldn't come to, then you just had to be sane enough to think. If they saw your thoughts, you were no longer on board for you to see. Up the street.

We were all living in an advanced world. This world and lifestyle all happened with phenomenon. Phenomenon. The phenomenon happened but not with fame, but with money. But with money. The money came from the street. It is truly remarkable how many things are made and how. They each go through a hundred-step processes. Thousand-step processes. Everybody gave up candy. After the UFO touched down, I witnessed and I disappeared. "Disappeared."

Prosperity. I was in the middle of some jungle Hijinx. "People were terrified, scared to death by others." Scared to death by others. People running everywhere. Abandoned, far cry, down, up the street, everything.

I watched a man with a shopping cart run past me, going from my left, going right. "Going, thinking really scared about a faceless figure I was, from out of sight from my peripherals in front of me to my left in front of me in sight of my peripherals to my right. Peripherals to my right. He was just hustling, jogging, pushing this shopping cart past me, and I saw his face. His face." I thought about looking at a man. When I saw this man's face faster than he could get by me but not before he could pass, I stood up because I saw him. "The shopping cart jinxed me." It would have indicated a joke. Although I wasn't crushed by the cart, I wouldn't be sitting down while a man jogging while pushing a cart passed me, pass me.

And before I could get up, there was another person there, a woman talking to the man rushing by me with the cart. She was thinking about him, the shopping cart madman. "The shopping cart madman." She was telling him to look out for me, just another careful pedestrian, because I was in his way she could see. She could see. I was a little enthralled by the whole thing because I was wrong being put there, waking up in the middle of something. It was not my fault. It was not my fault. I was ungrateful to have that happen, because I wasn't ready. I saw. I waited until everyone left. Everyone left. The planet was a specific shape. A specific shape. The aftermath, I really wanted that to happen again, so I went back to the area to set up what I already did, to correct it. I wanted to do it again. I inspected it and said, "She would show up for a rearrangement or not?" Arrangement or not. "I found that was most unlikely, to ask a woman to tell a shopping cart man to watch out for me again in a controlled environment." In a controlled environment.

I inspected the place and said that the arrangement for the woman to come and see something I did in the past again and it was that, or buy out companies and companies worth until things started happening again just as it would if you saw enough of something, or like it might be if you fell into a black hole. First, I bought out the land and took pictures of it. I then logged on to a computer to see if AI, artificial intelligence, knew about where he was, the shopping cart man. I then asked the AI if he could track down the man who was there when I stood at the wrong time again. I told him, "I don't want them to show up. I want the same thing to happen so I can stand up and take off at a certain time again, to fix what happened for my mind. I wasn't ready at the time when everybody rushed by. I want to correct my mistakes and stand up sooner."

The robot agreed and said this is how it's going to work. I got money ready to buy out a company, and I got the robot to set up an arrangement to ask the woman if she wanted to do something again. She agreed and said, "Sure."

We had a spy ask the man if he wanted to repeat something he'd done, and they'd pay handfuls of cold, hard cash. I was listening, and he said, "What?" The spy said, "Walk past a man who you saw before with a shopping cart." The man said he could do that again. The spy said to come by at this place at this time. He said okay.

The robot informed me that he got touch with the man, who was coming, and the woman, who would stand right there for the incoming show, in her place. She too said sure.

I bought out the company, and the woman saw everyone leave. I ran just before she could see me so the same thing did not happen to her. She saw me, already standing, and I rushed into place just before the shopping cart man rushed into place. The man with the shopping cart saw me rushing in just before he was in position for the stunt. "For the stunt." And when I saw the man walking toward the cart, I was already up. The woman who warned that the shopping cart man was coming at me just laughed and then smiled. Upon doing so, she only thanked me, because she did not have to warn the man I was there. When I was in position, just as the man passed me, I left walking backwards so that my actions did not affect the woman there by standing my guard. I walked backwards so that the shopping cart man did not have me breathing past his neck after the whole experiment. When he passed, I saw his face. I asked everyone to stay, if they liked, and I left. But upon leaving, I realized the impact this experiment had on their lives. They left too, and we weren't getting in each other's way.

I thought about the treason they were discussing, and I saw a beat up body with a bent neck in my mind after what they were discussing. I saw. Treason. It turned out that the more I thought about it, the sicker my thoughts became. Beat up bodies. Imagine that for them, is what it meant. I thought treason when these thoughts were about the conversation. A long time ago there was a body. "Body." It decayed, and the arm fell off. I was disgusted at how these people were talking. But they never stopped to think about the pictures it made in the mind, so I made my own.

When I heard certain things, I saw if I could think about it without hurting myself in my head. I thought about them. While they were talking and while I was thinking, if I thought, it would be like kissing him in my mind if I made a thought to their conversation. While they were talking. And I stopped to think about their words. It was a kiss. I only imagined. The treason was so that making it, thinking about all their words, would be like telling a sick joke. So I imagined what was good for this conversation: killing them. "I killed them in my mind only." When I heard, there was nothing to make a deal out of. I left a thought. I cut out when I heard treason. "When I heard treason."

Then I grew a mind. I fought them by imagining death and horror when I heard their conversation sound like treason. Like saying, "Here is what you are talking about … take it." If I made those thoughts in reality, I would start a fight. So when they said everything else that didn't sound like treason, I saw if I could make it. They were only thinking about it, because nothing happened. So I cut in. They were only thoughts, after all. I cut in between words, suffixes, and prefixes. "Suffixes and prefixes." This got even worse. I cut in this conversation in a theoretical make of what's to happen. What's to happen. When I thought about the treason, I walked away at average speed to see the world. I was done spying on them. My thoughts of fighting weren't good enough, so we took them into custody.

The TV turned on by magic. "When it comes down to it, Sleeping man isn't the only thing that is doing it." Sleeping man. "One thought." Thought. "Sleeping man." Sleeping man came from a man's thoughts. "Just simple, a thought." That's what sleeping man said. Extravagant or big, it was nothing. If it were big, extravagant, then it had chances. "A man wanted peace, so he went to bed, lazy head. This idea struck the world. A best-selling phenomenon." Couch. Phenomenon, world-wide selling.

The play is the best. Records flew from the shelves into gaming systems like magic, off the shelves into play systems. The world-wide phenomenon is called Sleeping Man. It started with an idea as simple as a joke, then grew into a multi-million-dollar-selling game. "Phenomenon, sleeping man." They grew into fully formed thoughts, because you were given an idea, and the idea grew from playing Sleeping Man. "Sleeping Man." Sleeping man. The Sleeping Man, said. The idea said, "Idea. Sleeping Man." The idea came from Sleeping Man, a game that one should play if they wanted to sleep. "Just a few seconds and you are asleep." Sleeping man.

Succeed. "I was scared my first time at Halloween, being out. Scared. I was scared because I was at my first celebration, my first Halloween I was at, and that is why I was scared." Why I got scared. It was like I was all alone in a crowd of people, all surrounding me in a circle, while they all knew why, everyone in order thoughts all random. Thoughts all random. Like I wasn't there, while they all knew each other and me. But I didn't know any of them. And me. Ignoring me while they surrounded me, paying attention to the arrangement of people. They edited things. "Arrangement of people." I left to see the world, because I would not stand for letting my fears go by. I left. I needed to be scared, like having a disease. "You need something?"

I found my fears. "Fears." I wanted to stay scared. "Scared." Scared. I got scared from the ceremony. I was at the back, and I was looking down at the floor. "Looking at the floor." People chanting. "Chanting." They were praying, a low hum. A low hum. The ceremony had people praying, while some in a low voice tone. Low voice tone. "You could hear humming." I could see their lips moving, their faces moving. There were so many prayers that my mind started to pray too, because of some of what I noticed they were saying. Like my lips were moving amongst others, praying from their lips, and prayers, like having a groovy song sung, like my lips, were moved by their prayers, and some were really praying about what I needed, which sounds like the work of the devil if you just listened. Listened. "Prayers." They were praying about my needs without knowing it. They prayed about what I needed, and one day or another, I would pick up those needs they prayed for. "They prayed for." Wouldn't it suck if you saw them at the market looking after what you needed after praying for it?

The prayers sounded like humming from so many people talking, but they were really praying. Talking. "A person humming looking straight at you, eye to eye." You could see. "People were posing, palms touching one another of their own hands, like a prayer for Jesus. They were praying." This hum created a forcefield, and you could hear everyone across the land singing words to this hum in your mind. "You could see bad kids getting bothered by skinned and burned girls, by their faces. Their faces were skinned, burned, and they were smiling at you, interrogating you from within their minds and intimidating you in reality." The hum. "They were hugging a hoody, like playing peek-a-boo and showing their skinned faces. From burns, they smiled to you."

Chanting, everyone was hypnotized, and their bodies were singing outside, while within everybody could see. "The picture I was looking at was at Halloween; the picture was looking at me." The glimmer of paint like eyes, looking at you. Eyes, looking at you. "I was trapped behind this picture at Halloween, although I never showed up for Halloween. I took off from fear of losing my fear, yet I was still at Halloween." Halloween. The land was blanketed in Halloween. Everywhere was scary, and the biggest effect yet was the hum that hypnotizes you to fall asleep. "I changed it by chanting, and other kids all around me chanted with me until everyone was covered by incantations. The hum."

Everyone in the Halloween land was chanting at Halloween; everyone's eyes were closed. When they saw bad kids, they woke them up and saw others whose faces showed they were all asleep. "Surrounding them. Chanting. They were not allowed to hear the real song." I must have been there first. Everything surrounded me. The trees and plants walked over to cover me up. The picture I looked at contained me in it, and I was moving, doing something. I never recalled that. "While it was showing off its guts, the paint smiled like shimmering eyes, a painting looking at you, or a laughing face. This picture also contained a secret passage." It was like the painting hugged you.

All other times, "I noticed it, after. I recalled everything that happened in my life, all the way up to how I got there. Within the picture I was led into a theatre going down vertically ninety degrees, into darkness. The building led me down into darkness." Everyone was there to see a movie. Once upon a time in a movie. Then everything blinked to swallow my body, and I was then surrounded by special effects, and I could feel my body clamouring with fear as the sweat of my palms clamped my fingers shut. I could see them shaking and I could feel the power of me shaking.

Then everything blinked, and I was gone from there. "Even me." These eyelids swallowed me whole, blinked, and battered me. "Or so it seemed." I really was warped into zoning out, and it felt like I'd left, but in reality, everything changed. "Everything warped like living dancing trees surrounding you in the woods or the meadows." The building was warped, twisted. The changes in reality were of nature by light, like a man with glowing eyes from under a light looking at you, seeing you. Like watching a bug walk away, a baby ant. "The light was shining, and so to it everything must have been moving, like dusk from midnight. Everything changed into dawn." Into dawn. Reality was alive. "The days and nights connote moving, because you could measure light by this movement. Structures were alive."

I wasn't hurt, but I was hurled into a universe posturing me being dead, and everyone else being dead too. I was hurled, by black, like falling beside the sun into darkness; everything was alive. "Everybody thought the more I asked, they were dead too." I then ditched to wind back to a secret passage. The passage talked to me, I could see it. "It was. It was secret because it showed me something that only I could fit through at the time. The walls danced. It was an entrance, a secret one too, beside the falling sun." And furthermore, how I got there winding back with my eyes shut was inconspicuous, like I was crazy, like I went for a little walk. To me it was inconspicuous. "The inconspicuality was that the word 'inconspicuous' was dancing, waving back and forth and showing me something." It was at Halloween, because who wouldn't want a painting with a secret passage inside the art? The painting looks at you; those could be your eyes. Weaved into a paint.

A man in a mask who is invisible underneath the robes. A candle lit with a finger beside it. "Finger, beside it." I was really thinking about what was at Halloween, though. "From a theatre to the middle of nowhere, I was watching the screen. Death struck at Halloween, death peeked. I witnessed this apparition commit suicide. Like others would follow, wearing this suicidal shadow. It was a Halloween imposter who tried to take Halloween with it. Skinned, an imposter tried to take Halloween with. Halloween may not like that; it likes people being dressed up. He dressed up."

Dressed up, Halloween smiling. Dancing round the place, he could have easily picked up speed. They were singing with no lips or humming. The ceremony was a sight to scare people. They gathered around to consume Halloween, so that you can know what it wants. From a fire, you could see a distorted face within it, being catered to, as more wood weighed heavily into it. Distorted, like the look of evil that has grown into a minion, with skin grown across its face, like hell. They were led wrong by this being's distorted face. One man danced out of the way into the right from his point of view, to welcome the planet. He danced forever. "They put away their drums by neatly folding them up in the grass and wheat, which was so much force that it sanded the drums into thin air, like invisible hands instrumented the drums and drum sticks. They took off their clothes and stretched and flexed until they disappeared into the clouds, into nothing, invisible. All who thought about Halloween saw this, even the distorted man's face."

"Halloween." I was thinking about Halloween. But in reality, Halloween was thinking about me. "It smiled." Forever went by, and it went by, like I was waiting for Halloween. It smiled, and the smile did not quit until I walked by it. Halloween smiled. "Forever. Like waiting in Halloween on a rainy day. Rainy days are for haunted houses." Rain, waiting for it to come, and while you were waiting for Halloween, Halloween was waiting for you. "You were standing at the edge of Halloween into yesterday, watching the light hit the earth from the other side of the planet. But not that beautiful, though. Because anything too beautiful would trigger responses that you saw Halloween, and you would no longer be waiting. Last night I saw the light. A dim light that lit up the night like a firefly; you could see glowing in your eyes, a firefly. You saw glowing eyes. A light flickering out, dim. Only in light I saw the night. I saw. They were there to spook each other out."

There to spook each other out. Doctor Pathic. One jumped out to scare the other from cover, by the wall, because he saw him, and the other showed a scary face to the other while running away, looking backwards. "The scary face you could see from your mind as though it is looking right at you. Face to face. One thought, without smiling in thought, you smiled in reality and not in thought. The other jumped out to scare the other because it was Halloween. He jumped out and behaved like an old man, to see it." Glaring. "You could see someone smiling."

Old man. "Old man." What happens in the night? I tailed Halloween, who was with many different faces, hidden inside the clothing. He was wearing a costume, covering many different faces. "Halloween was not meant to have its faces shown."

I took down my hood and screamed after I saw that. So they all pulled their hoods away all at the same time to reveal Halloween's identity.

Halloween. "When they arrived for the celebration, they triggered off the props, and before they knocked on the door, I spawned from a machine. From looking at them, from within, I could see darkness inside of eyes … hollow within, not through the eyes. Like, if you tried to take Halloween away from them, they'd kill. The machine I spawned from was hooked up across the grid electricity it was working at. You could see peeking." When the electricity was tripped from the prop outside, "I was notified, by a sight in my mind, because of the weight of everything, like a finger tapping on your shoulder, but the next second when you turned around to look, there was no one there. I was in stasis in a robot, after all, like falling into liquid fear, or just water. Like a lamplight flickering dim in the distance. This sight was really a prop going off."

The robot can read this sight by weight, it sensed. The robot you could see peeking around the corner, but then when you looked, the robot stayed there like nothing moved. The next second you blinked, and it was gone, pulling its head back from around corner. When I was about to be encountered by trick or treaters, I was taken by surprise and ran out the door. "Ahh!" A real scream. "You could hear. People without faces, under hoods." The robot, it seems, you could see his peeking face. It was so advanced, it controlled my mind by playing music so loud and far that everyone was hypnotized, and it rumbled the ground beneath my feet and tickled them so that I opened up the door and took off out to scare those worthy enough to see my house of the robots. I was dancing for the robot. Why I was dancing, Halloween. The robot.

I fell back asleep to wait for the next trick or treaters. The robot folded up into a teleporter and sucked, me back into the machine and turned off the lights so that I would not go insane from sleep into stasis, light shining in your eyes. I worked out and fell into stasis after I was buff enough to disappear to walk fast as a shadow person. I saw and walked away. "You could see the shadow wobbling back and forth, walking away." Flickering in the candlelight.

Lottery. "I'm psychic, but only to myself." I saw my face in my mind. I could see something peeking. "Any face, I could see in my mind. Hopefully they don't peek. Halloween stepped up to see what I looked like. It looked like Halloween."

It peeked. The face looked like a monster, peeking. "I moved around to get to the street, like a person scrambling. I was moving around on the street." You could see my bones flexing my muscles. My muscles flexed, and I hold up my bones. I was doing it; I was in. "From dusk into the night, the sky went dark; it smiled, and the clouds showed. They were moving and revealed a smiling face." It winked. "I think about going out." I wanted to go house to house to haunt people for candy, but I could not, because I had no body. I thought, *Head over there and crash their houses like Halloween did.* Halloween.

The witch peered in. "Of course, there was a party everywhere in the streets because it was Halloween." I thought about going in the night, I thought. I thought about scaring every one of them, I thought about. "And I couldn't just show up; I dressed for the show, in a split second, to be dressed for the show." My body was somewhere, a few kiloton million light years away, on a different planet, in stasis. I tried it on to be dressed for the show. My body was on another planet. If it weren't, then I would have to build it again by flexing, which is like learning how to walk again, chemotherapy. Flexing. I was not debilitated. Learn to walk. Alone on this planet. "It was like the night, who played in my dreams. In my dreams. I showed up to this house."

I wished. "I thought about my body moving around to get out of stasis on that planet, a few kiloton million light years away." Like falling beside the sun, forever. "It worked out until it dissolved out of stasis because I thought about it doing that. I thought about the body, and the body responded that my thoughts were not all there, as a joke. I then thought about where it was, I thought. My mind showed me a picture." I was not debilitated. The picture was the location to where my body was spawned to darkness long ago. I opened up a hatch. My body did. "I thought many things, and my body did them. I thought about everything in my mind, and I awoke from stasis. I had a memory of friendly faces and cool buildings. I saw faces in my mind. I remembered them just like Halloween remembered them, peeking in.

I remembered time from another, life ago, because that part of life, that scene, was perfect, so it was remembered forever.

I remembered them from my home planet. They were not what you expected them to be on this planet. The night took off across the vast black of space, a kiloton million light years away, and I remembered advanced life. I was invisible when I arrived, stasis. But visible I would be no more. "Only in dreams, or a robot, I would take visible. I would take robot hourly to the vision. Of course, going to a distance like that would be nothing telepathically because we can imagine space like that much more vastly than we can see." But space exaggerates much more than we can see. One look into the telescope and you'd know that you would be old if you traversed the space in between you, the telescope, and then or there. On this world. "I looked into the black of space."

Did you know that it would take you a kiloton million years to reach that point in space time? Space, Time Travel. "That is why they do things the way they do. And my mind was put into stasis so that I could use the body when I keyed my mind." My mind looked like muscle, like someone tugging on my shoulder without me looking. "I was awakened by this call from me. And why?" Because I would not be able get to Halloween without it. "When travelling like that, there is no rest. All that I've been saying." Of course, I've been thinking of all I've been doing. "I could see that I was awake on this planet, and I was ready for Halloween. I was going to haunt every one of them. After I haunted everyone of them, I was going to haunt the world." You looked into the screen, at the action going on. "You saw a man looking up." Screams. "I haunted the world."

The weight. "The weight of a brain. You saw it." My brain, I was thinking about my brain when I saw it, like watching your moving body in the mirror. "My brain peeked while and when I looked." You could see a brain in your mind; it looked like a brain, a well-marinated roast with spices holding the muscle in. "Out of body experiences, you saw what fear looked like. I saw it." My brain. "When I was sick before I was born, from the future into the past, I got a look at my brain. Sick." Sensory perceptions. Mind inside of a mind. "Does not work." Only works if you teach it. Teach your brain to a be certain weight, a mind within a mind. "Brain matter." Teleportation. A different time in space. "By playing with your mind to see if something fits should be where you would get the exact weight, which changes ionically when subjected to certain thoughts." Certain thoughts. "You worked out your brain." Telekinesis, Halloween.

Brain Matter.

"Live, in peace." You could see a bald man tell a story. "Work hard. A dark Halloween." They went out to get trouble. "They had feelings, if people weren't enthused by the stories. I investigated to see what was bothering them the most. I saw. When I was finished," everybody on this planet should be able to live in harmony. Why? "Because Halloween lived past it's day." It lived and would go on forever. Forever. "I then went house to house to see if they were living in peace. The speaker phone, I made. Across the land, people I spoke to were living in peace." People spoke. "Living before dying if they ever would. Work hard, and you could sculpt yourself an alien body by working out hard." Stasis.

Everybody disappeared from their houses and broke down the walls to make advanced ships, and they kept their costumes on to flirt with the night on the land in the distance. "They finished trick or treating, and the houses were folded up into the land, which sanded them into dust and then into nothing." They all stopped thinking and opened their eyes to the spirit of Halloween forever. You could see someone open their eyes. "And Halloween blew out the lights, from the light, out into the night flickering, into day." They thought about everyone behind, with Halloween. "They travelled intergalactically to stay with Halloween, forever." Around the planet and then through a wormhole at a star gate. "They added mass until the day shortened into night, the night of Halloween."

Everybody was then stopped by Halloween, a man tapping on your shoulder, and they dissolved into the daylight, light of day, for another time to come. They were at peace, and others from a different time landed to inherit Halloween for the last time. "They saw." Nuclear summer.

"Trick or treat!"

Trick or treat! "He was thinking about going to Halloween. A distant land, beyond the clouds, and in heaven through time and space to an inhabitant's future the same weight of your past." A man showed up from across the clouds and beyond the land and saw what it was like to survive. When everyone least expected it, lighting hit the land and you could see a tribal man walk out of the dust. "He walked away from a portal getting closer to the first person's view. Halloween, they took us to a play; there were hooded figures all holding their hoods like playing peek-a-boo when they got close to the middle of the circle. The portal exploded and was left with a short in the line. This is what it looked like in a play." In reality, he walked away to survive in the land he saw, by dancing and singing, and sanded into nothing. Then he arrived.

"He saw riches, bushes, berries all around. He left and harvested a land before he arrived here." He saw from there; he came from no peace. "He came from a storm, lightning; he spawned from the clouds, and lightning struck the land." You could hear from the ground bushmen singing on praise, of the survivors, arrival from the clouds indicating he is a saint. "You put your ear to the earth; you could hear bushmen singing softly." When we saw, we saw eyes, the singers were teleported to a distant land, the bushmen.

"You could hear music playing softly after being conjured into the clouds, the drums sticks hitting the land sanded into nothing." The gods danced out of the way; you saw shaking bushes, and the gods welcomed you in. "From the traveller who welcomed him from music and lightning, the gods were only there by imagination. The gods in my eye were travelling across the universe and back through loopholes programmed and built by engineering." They worked out frivolously to be born, from advanced communities and into new ones, by stretching and stretching and stretching into alien bodies and alien muscles from so much work. "They stretched and stretched and stretched until they dissolved into a new society. The gods were there in likes of the beauty, the planet, and from war."

War. When they saw war, they slammed into the planet. "Spawning them into their society to give them what they wanted, to solve war, their peace. Their power, you could see the stars flicker." When everything they needed was over and they were happy, the gods danced and shook the trees in the land; wind blew into the hairs of trees, and gods ate all the berries from the bushes and blew away for their treat. Upon every arrival and retreat, they always left a pile of money for all to see. The people were allowed to touch the money, which scared the people. "What really scared them is that the gods would wrap you up and twist you round and round, feeling infinite zero g's, and place you back into your seat at not a second's notice."

The man stopped thinking because he was awarded the land. He listened to all that happened in history, and he saw that everybody disappeared. "Into the clouds. They disappeared" into the clouds. "He stretched until his body dissolved in the air over the oceans and up into the vastness of space, in between the heavens of the constellations." Space exaggerates far better than the mind could, because space is a lot steeper. The constellations all got sucked into black holes to die peacefully and be teleported to another point in space and time, a mere fourteen billion years ago into the past. The black holes stopped becoming black and opened up their first day, computers. And their first day was simply the light of stars forming into life.

"The Big Bang was their life; all across the universe, things lived and died, black holes remembered them, and they were remembered by doing things in the name of the universe. The universe was reborn in a story called, The Multiverse." A million other years, in the name of all those who were living, an infinite number of people dating back to your ancestors, they reaped the beginning. "Everything was forgotten, and pictures ruled the universe in a story. Yet to be experienced, but has already played." That day he arrived like this, conjured from everyone's thoughts and spawned by a smiley face in the clouds, near a massive bolt of lightning. "He took off into civilization at a running start." The bushmen.

"What, said for, wonders?" I saw a face peeking in. When I spoke that, the voice of an angel spoke in the name of my voice. He was serious enough. He was dancing backwards, drumming around a circle drum with a hand drum. Until the drum broke, then eventually the other one and then dissipated into nothing by taking apart the mess that sanded from the pieces into nothing.

They said for wonders. "They said that on the final moment of their speech." The speech was made in favour of the gods, landscapes, and music. They framed it and all danced into nothing for the world to see. Their final speech was, "The gods were thinking about going to that land, through stargates, around them, and through time. They stretched the body until it works out into alien muscles and then into nothing. A shadow cast onto technology." They stretched into nothing, shadow, pure muscle.

"Thinking, about going to Halloween." Halloween. It said for wonders. "They said in speech that acting it out would make the final scene." The final scene. "They were thinking about leaving, thinking."

"In a play, it looked like a bunch of people conversing, debating." They were singing.

Extrasensory perception. "I see. Words." Extrasensory perception. "The origin is ESP." The origin of ESP, is ESP. "To me, I am fully psychic. To me, myself."

"Crypt." Wonders. "Crypt." All who saw would, from this message, be heard. "Across the land." Be heard.

They said. "Fallen. They said."

Extrasensory perception. "Words. Sensory."

"Sang, the dead knew it. They would whisper secrets to me when I turned the music all the way up." It was so peaceful that you would fall out of the sky like an angel fainting for art. "Fainting from the sky." They would whisper in my mind, a lot like putting a picture there in life, in reality. "Picture. I screamed across the land." Screams. They'd be rolling over in their graves right now. "How could they know? Because I knew." You saw my face. "I sang, and my music was played across the universe, like notes jumping into black. Money. Rich." I saw.

"I thought about the music, dancing notes, and realized that when I recorded it, at least it was playing in the universe, somewhere." In the universe somewhere. "You saw. The multiverse was over. The infinite stories that made up the multiverse were over for the eternity they were played." Forever, eternal. You could see. "And an old story began, one that was never played or repeated or sung in history." An old story that has never been played. "You see." But, happened once, on the notion that it never actually took place as a real event in history." History. "But it was so, that they at least imagined these infinite stories."

—Infinity

"The universe is old. You could see trees walking away. That's how old the universe is." So old, you would never make it across the universe, due to the universe expanding, darkness. Black. "The universe would tell you he's lost too." You could see something peeking, like a shadow peeking. "It was the only story, never to be repeated in the universe, but we repeated it. Even though it was forbidden." The gates to origin were about to open. Functions. I had it. My sense of time was with stasis. But that was before I felt like I lost my mind." I got to my maker, and I was gone. "I saw that I could not move by function. My mind still worked and only let me record this message. God, I wish I knew where I was." I was thinking about being here, but never that I lost all motor perception. They were messing with reality or something, because if they messed with me, I would have loaded all nines into them. They weren't messing with my real sight. Lost in space, Time, and Infinity.

They knew not where I was, but they knew something was about to happen. They made it. "Just outside stasis. The window in, and from, space, stasis." They made it so that when people got lost, they gave them something that they could recognize, like a toy; if that's what they pointed to, they noticed." They saw a young man lying there. He needed help as soon as possible, and while he needed help, power left their knees for not helping, so they picked him up for help. The Siphon.

"There was a man standing in the corner." Inside of a field house. "You could see that someone was speaking from nowhere, but you could hear." You heard music, then your favourite song. "This music was blasted so loud that you fell asleep." And when you fell asleep, you heard your favourite song! "They wanted me to wander into a crypt, and I would know because everything would then be seen from third person view when I entered this crypt. Like standing in a corner for a time out, only you weren't there for a time out and those corridors were rich. You could see your back." Crypt. "Phase two, inside of a crypt. You discovered something, so you backed out of the crypt and into the light." Lights were turned on so brightly that they saw through your body to your thoughts." The lights were there to light up your mind so you could see. "Your mind was to be seen, because that is where you could obtain the gift for discovering something from within a crypt." Sight. "Crypt."

Everybody out! You could hear a man sounding like the General, only that wasn't the General. It was someone far scarier; it was the captain! "The closer you got to the bottom, but not for real, you had to face the captain." The man was standing there, thinking about Halloween, and he went there, through hell, so that he could stay. "You could tell by the burns on his hands. Hell." A shout by the captain. 'Very body out!

They heard it; they heard chanting. They heard it because I cast my music. I cast music in my mind. "The instrument." The instrument was not the same in the mind, just as the keys were in reality. "When you looked at them, the keys were out of shape." It was because you weren't playing an instrument. Right? "But that's not the reason to play the instrument." The instrument was acting, the acting piece to be played, my music; the instrument was acting the acting piece. "It was dancing. Acting." The music plays. I put the music real loud and sang from here to the sun. "I left copies, and copies of music there, and my original tapes. When I was finished with the music, I left mounds and mounds of cash there for the discovery, to be seen like a hangout or youth club."

I left my body there, corpse. It was not just any corpse; it was a decaying body that woke up to speak when rotten enough to move. "How?" I amped up the music enough so that with all the music it would have played, it would leave everything into stasis, to fall asleep; it vibrated and massaged the land. "It even let matter, money, sleep." Arrival. "When I was in stasis, I got up right away to secure my future on this ever-looking planet I arrived to. In stasis I stayed, in a black hole, beside the sun." I stayed inside of technology. "Inside stasis." That is like staying inside while outside is sleeping, vibrating music to the edge of the universe and back falling beside the sun. "Music lit up the land, ahead of the orchestra, and in stories too. The notes they struck were not alike to the sounds that were made by such effects. The notes were singing while the instruments were dancing. Stories they came out of, the music matched. The notes would be low if they were seen sneaking around. They were thinking about singing while dancing. You could see their faces, and you could tell they were thinking about dancing while singing. Psychoanalysis."

"I saw everything from A to Z, alphanumerically." Said. "I saw." I looked to the skies, where I would be likely to catch a glimpse of what I wanted. How long the skies were. "I thought about how unconscious thoughts looked." I was thinking. Thinking alpha numerically.

"Alphanumerically." Thinking.

"They thought about thinking. They thought." Thinking. They were thinking. "Thinking." Thoughts.

"It was an opening coming from the technology outside, a robot within sanctioned the inside of the opening. You could see something peeking. It saw." Someone opened the door from the outside at one point. Like someone opened it without codes, then a ghost, wobbling through a wall to let himself in. "The codes were once holding it shut. Cracked it." A kid spawned from behind something, just as you'd see if you saw a ghost or a scary show. He was turned around in the play. It was recorded. "I came in and saw this mess of people's actions." Of what they were doing. "They were playing the technology. The technology typed in the codes to shut it down automatically, and the kid who spawned disappeared." Life was allowed to resume. "They saw his life."

They were like humans who wanted to see. They came out of nowhere. "I suspect it was the technology that was there. Everything was made of technology." And a reanimation machine was short-circuited. "I suspected by the arrival of everyone there, the short-circuited machine was actually rigged to spawn multitudes of people." Or people were sleeping in them and woke up to see life. "They spawned from this reanimation machine into stasis and woke up there like that." Reanimation.

They were beginning to scare people in reality. It was the start of a long tradition. "I went to sleep on my home planet. The robot was sleepwalking to all the places I thought about while travelling to ensure my safety, on the planet I travelled to. I woke up in my mind, a false awakening. I took off my robot. Lay like the wind. I became like the wind. After a good long sleep, the robot chucked me out as crew of his own that he then wanted to sleep, to see what I saw when I slept and what I would be doing during my time awake. I had a television program that I could see when I was awake; it was what the robot was onto while it was sleeping, in stasis. It was a hardware copy of his mind. To open up the real copy, you needed to see a backdoor computer program then out to a black hole somewhere. "I folded up the advanced program and hardware into thin air. An aircraft was waiting for me."

I saw. "People were working, and they noticed me too." I got out of the way. "They were repaving the streets. Not working on sewers." I would have noticed the suggestion. "Down in a dirty pipe, looking up, that suggestion." I saw. I thought about the screen on in front of me. "I noticed the screen and saw that it had to be correlated to what I was doing if it were legal. It was, because I was only looking at a screen. "What I was thinking. I thought, and it wasn't what I was thinking. If what was on TV was what I was thinking, someone would get a beating because that would be like aiming a gun at me, just as they would be like working if they were working on the sewers." They weren't working on my sewers, plunging at my thoughts and watching me like putting something on, which was good. Working.

"I hadn't used my eyes before." They were closed. "I opened them." I flexed out my eyes so that I could catch a glimpse at my mind. I blinked. I peeked. "Because my mind thought about what I was looking at." I turned my eyes to what I was thinking about. I was in stasis, and when I got out, I was instructed by subliminal messages to stretch my mind out through my body. Wake up and stretch. Perform a motor task.

My body I was to flex so that I could stay awake for the best part. "Being rich. It looked like people everywhere knew of me, or at least what I was like, because no one was fighting, and everyone were participating in life, no treason. They only watched to see where they were going to, that they would make it to their destination." They lived their lives happily. This town didn't look that nice during construction, but at least we weren't at war; there was no war. "I noticed why they were thinking, though; they were in the middle of espionage. Espionage could be fun too." Just think about all the paperwork you have in front of you. Espionage. They were doing their jobs, but only one was using a style. In fact, it wasn't a style at all … it was a move! "He pulled fraud at this company to get money. That and he was already rich. I could tell because every corner to every style was being used, even this man of fraud. It was funny, though, because he even paid the company so that he could work for them, but not with those people they wanted him to work with. He wasn't to tell them that he would migrate a yard to work with others." He was thinking about repaving the streets.

"The person whose mind was near the TV was watching the construction, and when she got bored, she went inside." She checked the TV and it was the construction people working just outside her house. This TV revealed to her that she could tell what people were thinking. She became rich. She shut the TV off, folded all the gadgets she had, and used them until they wore down into the size of a mind, which is nothing: a cell phone, TV, computer, a butterfly knife, and etc. "She wore down everything she owned. And stretched and flexed until she was put to sleep, from being too comfortable." The life she lives.

"Crypt." Wandering into a crypt. I wandered into a crypt. Where or why, I don't know, like exploring space across the galaxy and universe. I was lost and only knew how to walk, so I wandered into a pathway, one into a crypt. "The crypt was a horizontal corner, like a diamond shape facing you at a ball diamond." I knew it was a path to a crypt because I inspected my feet—that and I was able to walk, so it had to be. I wandered into a crypt. That I could see not past my feet, and what I stepped on was malleable when I flexed, so I knew how to walk and easily walked on pathways—the one I was standing on and one going into the crypt. "I knew how to walk, and when I went into the crypt, I automatically knew about because of a pathway. I knew the pathway like I could walk."

I made the point clear to myself. "I made money, though, because others thought about this place being haunted and randomly paid a would-be wanderer to walk into the crypt." To make contact with the real crypt, you wander into the corner and let the vibrations of technology take your soul for a walk. Soul for a walk." Soul for a walk. By walking into this corner, it automatically triggered music so loud and so melodious, with neural vibrations, that it put you to sleep so far into your mind that it awakened you from across the universe. "It is like going to sleep and flying to another galaxy millions of light years away from where you are, seeing those thoughts from when you thought about that point in space time and going there."

They lined up. Remember, that point in space time would be so far that you would die if you travelled there many times through space in real life. There was too much gravity there, so it pulled everything in. When I slept, I was there right away because the music served as a partner to let you sleep peacefully, peace, music. "This crypt is the foundation of this city." This crypt is used to direct movies. "On the other side of the city were the catacombs." They led all the way to other hotspots and crypts near this place. "This crypt is the foundation of the city." These crypts were used like safety deposit boxes or vaults, catacombs, and tombs. "Graveyards, or secret bank accounts, or sarcophaguses, or chambers." This is why it is used to make movies, because they were mysterious.

"They found a new way of doing things every day." That and when people were lost, they were given money or items they knew so that they could find their way back by building a past or future, or their homes and what they used to look like. "Even I took the way out, an object something, one I recognized. It was better than being lost and feeling lonely." That and I was born in some advanced community. "Born in an advanced community."

The bees were thinking about swarming life. "You saw." Beehives. "Bees buzz to make noise, and their minds are empty like the exoskeletons they have on. They can see the outside of the universe through interaction of the eyes they have with light shining within, prisms." Beings like me have endoskeletons with skin around and can see not through our minds, but we are the opposite of through eyes of bees, because we can see through our skin and eyes around. We have no exoskeletons. Bees have exoskeletons, so they can see by light entering their eyes and shining like prisms, not like the eyes human beings have. "Bees and their exoskeletons."

"Everybody out!" The Captain yelled. The Captain.

"They did." They did. They said.

They came out of nowhere. "Interception." Interception.

Feet. "His feet."

Feet.

"His feet."

I was going. "I thought about an evercraft." The story that controlled my life. "The evercraft was about a story." Ever craft. "Like a brand logo." Evercraft is merely a made-up situation. "It is made up, but it is really just an object used to get out of trouble." I called it an ever craft.

In the right place, people were talking. "Talking." Everglades, were coming forth as forests in trees were about. They were talking because of mischief. Hiding under cars that weren't theirs. "People of mischief." They were playing comic books. You could see someone tear out a page. I was going. I wanted to play. "Like homemade water slides." They were outdoors having fun. They disappeared and one was left; you could see smoke surrounding one's body who by smoke disappeared. "They screamed." You could see one with his mouth open, yelling. One was hiding, and

I could see. "Saw his feet." They turned on a light and one was gone, vanished. I'd seen his feet.

"I recalled being in a room where the lights were on but none there." Like a rich ghost wrapped in red silk, holding it up like putting on a cape. Holding it. "He waited." Like waiting on the street for a bus. And waited. "You could see the face of a clock." I flushed out the hiding kid almost as soon as he disappeared. Disappeared. When he disappeared. "I checked out his feet to see if that was him; it would have been obvious if I'd seen his feet." I checked out his feet where they were when he turned on the light. He said, "I was thinking about my feet, that's why you could see my feet with the lights on. All I would have to do is think about my feet, and it is similar to objects lifting up and being underneath them." —Telekinesis

Eyes were looking out, "Eye balls." One with pink in the corner looking in this direction, and the other looking a like an eyeball more than ever. "Humming." I could tell that they were thinking because eyes were looking, like being from a painting. "The eyes were wet." A wet painting, like someone just painted the eyes. "They were peeking at you."

A thought. "I could tell what he was thinking, and I found him; it was his feet because they were sticking out, and he said, "When I thought, I thought about my feet because the house was fixed, that and the light switch was rigged. I had to think or do. I couldn't see anyone, so I thought instead. My feet." A dirty foot. "I found him, and his feet were the clue." A mouth open, ready to speak. "His feet were the clue, and he would have hid in plain sight for me if he wanted to be found, in a real hiding spot." Reality. "But I guess it's his game to be found. But the fact remains, they were in my house at my yard." They thought about his feet, because his feet were there. There. His feet were of the Everest mountains to be seen because of a rigged light switch. Sticking out. They caught up to him. "The Everest. Twin glades." Twin glade. "The mountains."

The height was comparable to the vastness of space. Like following a shadow that would not stop but never leave you behind. Like a friend. "Looking straight up." The mountain peak sliced through the clouds. "The foot of the mountain." The foot of the mountain. "Mountain." The mountainous everglades. They were showing the mountainous regions. "They were showing regions." The exaggeration was his feet.

"They showed because they were the highest, like a mountain like a good joke." If you ever wanted to mess with the joke, you would head up to those mountains and pass a mountain peak where the shrine of the joke rests. "That and you'd feel joked if you wandered that far up." Otherwise, enjoy thinking about the joke, whatever latitude you wanted to think about the joke, whatever exaggeration you were, or are at. "The joke, a man laughing, his mouth open."

I checked out these regions and found that they were similar to how gods react. Snow on a stone pedestal. They were in high places, shrines to the joke, and when I glanced to the clouds, there was a cigar floating in the clouds. "A UFO." I was gazing at it for some time, trying to make something of it. I flexed my face. I didn't know what to make of it. "They picked up and left to the everglades. Pack for a camping trip, the mountains." I had a chance to mess with the joke. "I caught those poor sons of bitches before I left for the everglades by following microscopic evidence seen from my mind." I asked if I could see it or not, and if I experienced this before. "It came down to it that if I experienced this evidence before, I would know what to do." And if I didn't, then it would come down to it that they did it. "I made sure I had a chance to mess with the joke, like I knew what to do." I suspected that this microscopic evidence belonged to the gods, and it was mischief because of the gods siding with kids, but kids hiding behind gods because they were kids." No one was harmed, because they put themselves in god's way. "They put them and safety first." That and they knew the joke was good, all the way up in the mountains. The joke was for business, not for pleasure. "That time I was out." Come forth to see. "He saw being bugged from years in advance, foul play, and told everyone." The more that people talked about this foul play that supposedly would happen, the closer the years got, and the more people talked, the closer it got, like gravity ripping things apart that didn't exist, making them exist, the stronger gravity got. "I caught up to them about the joke the old-fashion way." I trekked that mountain too.

Question? Where they came from, I don't know. "Where they came from, I don't know." They came from their minds after making it with all the tools you could think of. They had robots, but they were cartoons. "They ate and stretched and stretched until from within rambunctious behaviours, the joke they were born." Darting your head. "They ducked and hid out of sight. They hid behind one another's eyelids for the game, the game that lasted forever." Another hiding behind your eyelids.

"Feet. I looked at my feet. I thought about my feet." Thoughts of feet.

"I thought about tickling his feet but never got around to it." So I guess I tickled them in my mind. I thought about it twice over and it came from that silly game they were playing. "Tickle them in my mind." Mind. I thought about tickling feet. "Tickling feet."

"Foot." Feet.

The beat. "I was listening, to the sound of the beat, of binaural beats." The beats sounded like humming. "Drums." I could hear it. The sound of binaural beats. "They were intended to stimulate my hearing and mind." Massaging the inside of my shoulder blades. I could tell because if I fell asleep and thought a certain thought, I would twitch, much like massaging super tense muscles, much like having a hand between your shoulder blade and your ribs, massaging your bones. I saw. "I listened to binaural beats again." They repeated, a certain set of beats after a moment or two. "Like a double music beat." In order. I stopped listening to beats and stepped out of the way. The binaural beats instructed me to the dream I was in. "I dreamt the beat was ongoing through a tunnel, a tunnel full of lightning. Then I was at a maze."

Dirt down a maze. I noticed the maze was dirty, so I picked up after it. I thought about everything while in a maze. I had so much fun, like sliding down an endless slide; there were signs everywhere, a secret passage, a haunted maze hallway, outdoors, and an obstacle course. A minute, I could settle for hundreds. One minute went by just like that. The minute hand. "I remember thinking about the day. I remember thinking about the day before when I went to bed. I woke up thinking about the maze. I started doing things for real. I thought about my dreams, so I put myself in a robot so I could see. This place I wanted to see was in exospace, a place built to keep your mind at rest while you can still see, without going crazy, sleep. Relaxed. I finished cleaning this maze and found the exact location it was at, since I was only dreaming. I was only asleep in a robot, so my pass wasn't permanent. I stretched and flexed until my body dissolved. I was in exospace; I was with the maze. "I tailed him from the maze." I connotated the maze; I entered it and never came out. I went missing, and the maze was scared I went missing. "I never came out."

I knew what was up there. "They were up there." They came from the sky. "I was puzzled about what's up there." The sky was up there. My mind was fuelled to what was beyond the sky; my imagination was fuelled by the day. Where did it come from? "Where it came from, I don't know. Or I'd never be thinking about that right now." I only had wonder in my mind. "I woke up by my own thought, thinking about not knowing what happened. I woke up thinking about what's next because I didn't know what happened." What's next.

They. "They put an imprint on my mind. Glasses." It looked like looking through glasses. "They." I thought about leaving away from them. "I left secretly for all my money from an abduction. They abducted me."

"I thought about crossing the ocean because I was scared." The ocean is many kilometres deep, and thousands more vast. "Scared of having water run down your back." You could see a face. "I was scared of where I lived." I lived near a lot of trees. "I thought about crossing the ocean." I never did it. "But the time came, and I thought about me in a dance to the gods." A man humming prayers watching to see if others came continued to hum. "He was building something, a body made out of many ingredients and nutrients." They conjured and spawned everything. "When I looked, I was already seeing the waters receding to the other side of the ocean." Backwash. The vastness of the black depth of ocean. Conjured.

The ocean opens up. "There is a funnel above the ocean. You could see the other side of the planet. A rocky terrain. The other side of the funnel actually had microscopic particles dropping to and from the ocean. When it dropped, it formed new fossils called anymite. It formed new particles from the dropping particles. They ran up the stream and even through the waterfall, this microscopic waterfall. "Crossing it would let you think whatever you wanted." But doing, that's different than thinking, just how different they are. You thought about doing it. You crossed the ocean. "The ocean you crossed, and you travelled again." After thought. Crossing the ocean. You rewound the tape to make another trip. "You thought. You lived eternally there. I lived eternally there because I crossed the ocean." It was so peaceful that I crossed the ocean to let my mind fall into stasis, stay at rest whenever I wanted. Black depths, the current of wandering, ocean stream. Streams.

A man concentrating. I was thinking about telekinesis. "A man concentrating." It struck me to let it come true. "I wished. I couldn't understand what people were saying." I saw. I made out that they were talking. "Concentration." I was staring at them and came to that they were talking because I saw their lips moving. I picked up my stuff and left. A man shaking his head in acknowledgement. I came to what I was doing. I was working. "I saw." I hadn't spoke in a long time. "A man concentrating." I was used to doing instead of talking. I saw them talking. "Extrasensory perception, the beginning. Telekinesis." I slapped one of them in likes that I could get real telekinesis, something moving. So I slapped him to make sure he'd gone after me. The clothing was suggested by me that it was moving right? When he caught up to me, I told him I only wanted telekinesis. The power to make something move through the body and mind. I then said, "See that over there?" I pointed with my lips. I could tell that I was thinking about it. Since it was in thought, I said if I moved this after thinking about it, then telekinesis because there would be microscopic evidence proving telekinesis. Basically, I did something and it moved by fault.

Sitting, meditating. Mastering life, I was thinking. "My palms touching each other." I saw talking. I pointed my lips in that direction. "I was acting out what to do in my mind so that I would not screw up. I was rehcarsing." I started my adventure, and I was already done by the time I started. Why, because walking was the opposite of talking. And my concentration gave in.

What talking. A man talking. "I acted it out. I saw." I thought about this man's thoughts. I knew. "I knew which thoughts were mine in my head. Foreign. So foreign thoughts could not be mine." Or the streets. "They couldn't be mine. I would not want my thoughts being on the streets. If my thoughts were lying on the streets, I would pick them up and read them. Reading them would be like giving a beating." I was talking. I saw talking. Talking. But their lips weren't moving. I knew they were talking because they were talking about things they were carrying and looking at. "Looking at." Carrying something. I heard them because there were speakers. That and I had advanced technology. I was spying on them.

Drums. "Drumming." Drums to a beat. A man holding a drum. I saw. "War! I put my drums away and folded them up into the land; they sanded down into nothing. And I harvested the land. When I had all the right ingredients, I lit them on fire to cool space. And I blew up the sun to start a black hole, and I left to have everything rearranged: my thoughts, my mind, even my body. Everything. Time travel." I was sitting writing a story and did not stop until the book I was became enchanted. It lived. With enough of one thing, you could make anything. A book there. "Enchanted. I wrote a journal." I walked to get something. I was going to act it out in the name of peace. It didn't happen. One ran away to get something, and it didn't look friendly the way he left because when we saw there was peace, he left real fast. I quickly hid and did not know what to think after that. The thing is, I never used my ears before, and I used advanced technology to decipher everything. The tech I was using showed me how to pronounce. When I heard my machine pronounce what it said, it said, "I'm going to get a gun." I disappeared.

Man with a gun. War. "Espionage. Journal." I heard thought. "Thoughts." We no longer needed to talk; the land sang.

"They were singing incantations."

The drums beat. Incantations. "War. It was okay to sing, yes. Incantations. I muttered." I can see a man drumming. "The drums beat, songs, the sticks pick up with no one holding them." The drum sticks. "The beat you could hear." Invisible hands. Hands. Falling. "Everything fell. They made." A man making something, I said. "I thought. I put the drums away by folding up the land into dust, then into nothing." The drumsticks' beat. "I hear singing."

They were singing incantations. Singing. "The drums beat songs across canvas." Songs. I muttered. "This song you aren't singing." The drums beat notes across canvas. Incantations. It was okay to sing, yes. Incantations. I muttered. I can see a man drumming. "The drums beat songs across canvas." Sticks. The sticks pick up with no one holding them. The beat you could hear. Invisible hands. Beating. The beat picked them up. They made. "You could see someone making something," I said. "I thought. I put the drums away by folding up the land into dust, then nothing. The drumsticks beat." I hear singing.

My eyes peeked; I saw. "I was doing. Doing. I Saw." Something.

"Incantations." There was an old story. "Ballad of the wind, I said. Enchanted hymns. Singing." Songs I hear, singing. Instruments playing. "They were at a play, playing." I thought about it. And you could hear brain matter flex. I started thinking. "About talking. I started talking." It's been a while. I was talking.

Music. "A play. All the instruments were chanting." Ballad of the wind. "I saw talking." Lips moving. "Show off or listen." I waited. "Decision. I decided to listen." Eaves drop. I heard them singing; I was doing poetry. "I was eaves dropping." It looked like they couldn't "see." "Like a psychic. I had a machine that vibrated in between my bones under every muscle." It was peaceful enough to be put into a lucid state. Peaceful enough to see. I saw everything. Psychic trance.

Drums. Beating. "Before I said something, I forgot. I repeated to myself." Drums. "Those were my thoughts." Incantations. "I finished my walk." Magic, a ghost turned on my favourite show; you saw a pale face. "They were drumming." Using leather in their performances. "They sang. Their performance used a canvas drum." Canvas, drum. "I was walking away, showing something from the performance." A show and a drum. "Eyes peeking. I saw." Motor beyond control. I was doing something. "I appeared in the show, and the place was lit up." I talked to make it seem like I was enjoying the performance. Then shots. "I disappeared. I thought it would be a good time to leave." I was gone from the scene because I left. "Gun shots." I disappeared.

"Instruments mock the voice." They are singing, a song singing a song.

A face poked its head into the room. I saw. "I looked. Dancing, I said. I danced." I looked. Dancing.

I thought about dancing. Ballad of the wind. "In peace I showed." Out the back. I listened. "I wasn't really dancing. I was not performing, although I was dancing. It was a snapshot of peace, at the level of dancing." I started dancing. Me dancing is another me doing its thing within my mind that always happens at a point like that; the beat picks you up so you could hear it, and your soul dances away into the clouds, with or without you. Automatically dancing. When you hear something groovy, your soul dances with or without you.

I saw a man drumming. Dancing, a show. "I can see a man drumming with one hand, his right. His right." I peeked. I saw. Drumming, a show. "I started thinking, doing." Mix things up. "Then I folded up the land and took apart my drumstick." I put it away by folding up the land, grass, until the stick disappeared into sand. "I lit up the sand and it burned away, and I fashioned every thing into a machine that flew away. I put myself into stasis in this machine that dissolved me. Then the machine. I flew away."

Love for who I adorn the most, love I see. "Doctor Pathic."

You could see a wick lighting up like a laser. A stream steady enough like water, drawn when you took the tip away. A laser. Explosive powders. A steady stream. Laser.

"Singing I said." For the love of my life for who I so adored. For who I so adored. The love of my life. Doctor Pathic. "I folded everything up and neatly put it away." Everything got put away so that it sanded into nothing neatly. Numerically. I heard singing in the name of Love. I watched people who once danced away nothing. Shadows they were. Nothing. Into nothing.

"I said, looking." Look, you could see eyes peeking. Wet like paint. Glancing, peeking.

"Singing. Ballad of the wind," the wind. For love who I so adored. For who I so adored. The love of my life. Ballad. Love of my life, for who I so adored. Doctor pathic.

She was a beauty with long blonde hair. I loved her so. "Blonde hair." Long blonde hair. Doctor Pathic.

I saw.

"I seen."

"I said," upon doing something. I was up to nothing.

Ballad. Ballad of the wind.

I wrote a letter, and the letter said.

"Ballad of the wind." For who I so adored. The love of my life. "Ballad of the wind."

I ran because I saw something.

I see.

"I wrote a letter."

"Ballad." Songs, dancing.

I was a gunner in trenches. "Espionage." War! "They deserve it."

Stasis. "I was in stasis."

Ballad of the moment. "Ballad of the wind."

Ballad of the wind. "Heart." Out.

They were in stasis. "Stasis." Zero Gs.

They were in stasis, because they were in zero Gs.

They were in stasis. Stasis. "The drum is beating with one hand." One hand. "War!!" Paint. It was the point where everyone was asleep in zero Gs going a hundred knots. Going a thousand knots. "Beat. Long time ago there was a beat. Its rhythm was like a heartbeat. They were going many knots because they were in zero Gs." Stasis. "Stasis. The drums were folded up into the grass and then sanded away into nothing. Espionage." You were going a hundred knots in stasis, going a thousand knots. Drums no more. Many because they were in zero Gs. Drums beating. "Stasis."

At the start of the beginning of math. "Mathematics." Not philosophy. "Zero Gs." After zero Gs. "A walk." Walk.

"The music was tuned." Tuned. Tuned to "Sleeping man. Play sleeping man today!" A man was on an underwater ship. You could picture seeing a man sleeping with his face to the sky under an awning; from his right you could see under a home. Rain pouring down. It showed someone sleeping. On TV, in a theatre, I was interrupted by sleeping man. Tune the music. "When they expect Sleeping Man, they expect sleeping man today." The man sleeping. Sleeping to the sky. Sleeping Man. The show was showing they were interrupted by sleeping man, the commercial. Buy sleeping man. Play sleeping man today.

"Sleeping man." Sleeping man.

"An awakening." Awake. "A Wake."

"Ballad of the wind." Ballad to the wind. "Wind."

I saw someone going slow. Going slower than I could walk. Like a clown car, so slow that you could compare it to someone giving it a running start before booting it up. I couldn't see. "Couldn't see. I imagined going slow, walking." Like I would have caught up to a car. More like I was going the speed of that car in my mind. Walking by them. Looking at them. Looking at them. "Slowly passing, someone driving." But in a traffic jam. Traffic jam. "Stasis. I sped up faster than stasis." I was in a psychic trance, and my mind was intact. I was really dreaming. I started going fast. "Like I was walking on stilts. Up to a running start. To pick up speed." I was walking the speed of teleportation, and then I sped up, looking at my watch. My watch hadn't changed. "Time hasn't changed a bit. I was going the speed of light, the speed of a black hole. Racing by them. At that speed, things started happening. Walking ever faster than they could drive." Time travel. I checked out the future, the planet at that speed. I started at Halloween. In stasis. The more I imagined, the more vivid it became. I rounded the planet. Then the houses were transformed at the shake of my head into Halloween.

Stasis. "Stasis." Time travel.

Ballad of the wind. "Ballad of the wind." I looked up to the sky and saw an upside-down abyss, like staring into the deep in space.

I kept occupied every day until I noticed the unthinkable. "Everything transformed; the trees got so old they could talk. The sound of ballad of the wind. Sounds like this." I was walking fast. Slow like the wind.

Ballad of the wind. "Everybody stayed away. Espionage." Ballad of the wind.

It started like this; bombs awfully close to your head. Everybody stayed down and, luckily, I had my way. "Everybody stayed down." Stayed down. "Imagine a place with no war." No war. Ballad of the wind.

"Imagine a place with no war." Ballad, of the wind. I signed off. "Signed off."

"I had my way in war." Ballad.

"Ballad of the wind." Ballad.

War, "Stasis."

No breathing. I saw someone; I couldn't tell if they were breathing or not, because they were too far away.

A tornado blowing with shrapnel flying everywhere. "A bomb." A bomb resonating from the clouds like a tornado touching down, heaven, fiery tornado yet it was a nuke. "It knocked on heaven's door, from stasis." Hearth. "I woke up." Bomb. "Bomb. The whirlwind picked up." Ballad of the wind. Picked something up. "Something, picked up."

"Stasis." Espionage.

"The saucer came down from the clouds like this. The saucer." It lowered into a cloud formation. Cloud formation. "That didn't punch the clouds. Punch the clouds." The clouds pushed the saucer and it landed, hovering, because the reactors were on. The reactors were on. Espionage.

Saucers. "Saucer." Punched the clouds.

The fire. It started and travelled into the bushes, into the forest. The fire originated from the forest, radiating into the sky beyond the clouds like atoms were on fire. You could see a being from the backside of him. Naked because it was hot; you could see his ovular head, turned backside. Napalm. "You couldn't see. Except a lit up sky. You suspected an explosion and there it was, in the bushes beside the forest." In bushes beside the forest. "A glow." Separate from reasoning, you saw a glow. "Grey said."

Saucers. "The saucers came down from the clouds like this." From the clouds like this. "From the clouds, they dropped nukes into the culminating land; they started in lines of longitude, down the map here." They could only drop one per region because of the damage the bombs do, plus they the ones who deployed it would blow up." They gathered everyone up and left into and from a big flying saucer. They got scared, but they succeeded. They got scared, but they made it.

"Reason. Stake."

"Reason." Stake.

Everybody stayed down. "Bombs of welcome." Of welcome. Everybody. Bombs.

"I thought there would be reason to think."

And now there was reason.

"I thought there would be hope."

Hope.

"Everybody stayed down from the shock waves." They stayed down.

From the shockwaves. "The shockwaves, they stayed down." Shock waves.

There was reason to think. "Reason to think."

"They stayed down. Everybody looking." They stayed down. They all stayed down.

They. Looking. I saw the bombs. "They were great in numbers."

"Everybody stayed down." Who stayed down? "They stayed down. Because of treason." They stayed down. Down they stayed. "I was thinking."

Who stayed down?

"Everybody out!" the Captain screamed.

Whistling sounds you heard. This is why they stayed down. "Why they stayed down?" Stasis. Stasis is so peaceful that people could hear their own thoughts, and even perceived their thoughts from a source coming from beyond their minds. "Sounds that you could audibly hear, from your mind, like whispering." Whispering, stasis, you could hear.

They were thinking about the Captain until suddenly: "Everybody out!" Everybody out. The Captain shouted. They jumped out of bed, into their clothes, eyes wide open. Good morning, sunshine.

Everybody fled to see the action take place. They went down to get the bomb. "One mercenary flanked the flight and headed up the field we were covering." We flanked and recovered the bomb. "Flank and cover." He recovered the bomb. "Recovered the bomb. Bombs. Bomb. Recover."

Everybody out. "He shouted." The Captain. You could see other army members rise out of bed like Dracula floating out of his coffin.

They went down to get the bomb. "They went down to retrieve a bomb that was already set off." They boiled the land and picked an amplitude of shockwave to revert the already exploded bomb. A hydrogen bomb. They set off the tape and let it play while it rewound. The shockwave, they could perceive with the recording they played, they picked up, playing. Every spot that we saw that was ruptured; we picked up and rebuilt it. By the time we played everything, there were a span of computers and other hardware that played if they built it up in order; it would equate to a bomb going off in the distance, the reverse of it. Engineering, reverse engineering.

"Everybody out!"

Everybody headed up the field. It was the safest, where no gunfire was sanctity. They saw a hill. "Just beyond the hill, the sky; they headed up field." Sanctity was there up the hill. "Clear." The sky. Some members cried so hard when they saw the sky. They were free from enemy territory. They were sent home, a bush hike. By the time they hit the hill, they were safe from the middle of the mission.

"Everybody out!" The Captain shouts. You could see the bed heads laying in their beds, cuckoo, early risers.

One timer a shot in the dark. War. "Stasis." Stasis. They were in stasis. One was Halloween parading all the way from his house up to war, and everybody wouldn't cross Halloween for anything. Halloween was too good. So hiking, dancing all the way up to war was good.

Screams and yells, yells. "That's how it started." Halloween. And then. They were wrapping up the forest; they made so many items with the forest that took it down. This happened in just an instant because of the multitude of people there. "It looked like war. Imagine what you could do with the forest floor with the right knowledge." I tore into it until I made gunpowder, then I massaged it until I made C4. I blew everything up, and I floated away because there was war.

"The screams came from Halloween. The people from the forest took the forest down and drifted into stasis. The people from the town beside the forest built up from inside their technology and took cover. They hatched from the technology. Inside technology, deep within tech." They hatched. "The robots within chewed their way out from within the tech; they exited as others entered. They came in with ease. They put their things down." Others parked their cars outside. Each person had enough personal space to get rich, like owning a mansion. They never violated reality. That would be like standing in their spot, alternate reality. Because they treated space like money. Then they traded, and someone took the spot they went down to see, and upon trading, they owned it. They made more money by handling money while they were handling money. "They stayed out of each other's faces so that they could think whatever they wanted. They were there to think, and there to talk." They wouldn't get their way because people valued and guarded space like treasure. "So they stayed out of each other's way so that they could think whatever they wanted."

Think whatever they wanted. That C4 was mine, breakfast, an old saying. They were thinking about doing stuff to get even more rich. I climbed down from the outlook. The people from the forest used all their equipment to take the forest down. Then "They sanded their tools down with the rest of the land and took the valuables with them by paying each other into nothing. The people within the technology all broadcast their lives onto another planet than this one. When everyone entered, others exited in a perfect harmony. The others who entered had all their belongings sanded down into nothing, just like the others.

Fix. Fixed. Fixing. The fence was broken. "The fence was broken." I fixed it. First, "Dig into the ground to find clay and then mix it with a mechanical mixture of water then dust. Keep mixing until the mixture shows a step of nearly lucid mixture. This is surely C4. "The clay that was in the ground was harvested; the water was used to make the molecular structure of C4. They mixed it." Why they mixed it. "This, is surely C4." They mixed it to blow things up.

And we all took cover. "Why we all took cover?"

Technology is instant cover. Plus, we could engineer and program to entertain ourselves. To refrain from shell shock, post traumatic depression, etc.

Bomb day. "Bomb day." C4, night.

"They built out of stasis because it was their safest. And they erected skyscrapers for safety. One day, they would have space stations touch the ground down through the atmosphere." There were wires and lights coming from seemingly the floor. Out of nowhere. Why? Because everyone would make old leads and new splices. The technology was hooked in. "They picked it up and ravelled it around its power source, turning it nuclear some of them, fraying and ripping the plastic to load it into a plasma weapon. They broke it nuclear because it was easier than taking it apart while it was on. They ravelled it." It switched on. "It built the walls it tore." It frayed. The technology operated. "They took down stasis." Wires came from out of nowhere. They made old leads and new splices. More technology came from stasis. All the technology came with it wrapped in boxes, newspaper, wrapping paper. Because it came from nowhere, they used whatever they could get their hands on, and it came in all shapes and sizes.

There would be only wrapping paper to show as a piece of technology that people needed, and since it was everywhere, they did anything to get their hands on this tech. They ravelled it up and boiled it into weapons. Or took it apart as scrap, a UFO. Other tech came from a new land. They had nuclear technology, which turned on across the land instead of leaving a blank, the land blank and empty, like they thought up the technology and turned on. The technology left cavities of pure and precious metals. They danced away into the clouds. The space station touched the ground, a storm, hovering over lighting storm.

Safety. "Safety." Security. Misfortune.

Because of abandoned, everybody stayed down. Sanctity, purity. Misfortune. "Cover was sanctious."

When war happened, they took cover for good. You could see a man at first thought in the middle of war with his hand raised to the sky, covering himself, ducking. "It was permanent for the time they took cover." Drift into stasis, they said. Crew, everybody had their way and did anything to keep their eyes closed, asleep. And so to it, they drifted into stasis. Stasis. "Your mind is disconnected from reality, away from things that aren't true, and you drift into the weakness of space to cradle your body, to put you to sleep and dissolve your tissue into shadows forever. "Your bones in technology." (Your bones in technology.) "They took cover." You could see a man with his arm in the sky cover himself, ducking. They throw Molotov cocktails. They originated from the forest; they gathered and built it into stasis, and they tore up the land until it made gunpowder. Cocktails.

You could see a man building their shelter; the Molotov cocktail goes right over. They originated from the forest. Molotov cocktail. You could see a man sewing; he made tools with all his skill. Cocktail. The picture of sewing is there to keep you and him busy; what he reaped, what he sewed, he is a master craftsman. A long, long tale. You could see someone reading a book. Molotov cocktail. You sew what you reap. "The signs from the still water showed us what dreams are made of; they took off into the clouds. You could see a man talking." Into the clouds. "Talking." They built it into stasis because it was easier and safer around war. A vehicle being driven. Multitasking. "Throwing a Molotov cocktail." Overthrow.

Maybe in the devil I made business. "I became skilled." I scaled a roof on a planet. I grew up. "Stasis. Slow motion." They once stated that they could hook out of stasis and into a light that would explode if not made right; it exploded from being ground. I assembled everything and put gasoline in it. "The bottle." I put a cloth in there and let it sit. If they tripped the power the right way. Molotov cocktail. "They would have it ravelled up to correctly work with a light socket, bending and tearing the technology until it frayed bullets of energy if used right, or it would make a nice light or a welding torch if set right. You could see the torch. And into stasis they just turned it on instead, making an extra step; it was easier. "They flipped a switch." Someone talked. "If they did not originate from the forest, they had their standing technology from beyond the forest, a town." They used it to warp from out of stasis into cover, a mass the same weight as your past, without war, a different time. The same. Time travel. While just up the street, they were messing around.

A man covering himself without war, someone shouted. I saw my way out, the army. In tents, we went. They wrapped up the technology. "They build advanced weapons, cover, stasis. Cover." They tore, which powered the technology on from cords turning on, ripping the plastic from the force everything that was packed in. You could see cords sticking out; one of them was a clip. "They took their supplies into account." You could see someone talking, counting. Their supply. "Taking their supplies into account." Talking, counting. "While taking cover. You could see a man covering his chest up." They built advanced technology by frying the technology; they built by wrapping the wires up until the plastic and rubber around them ripped, sometimes making bullets and plasma rounds. A clip. "You could see a man in the distance, sewing. He made many with his hands, a master craftsman. They pulled the wires from the walls and soldiered the wires by its own power ground, the electricity within the wires." Messed with, soldiered. "And if done right, soldiered. Shot." The man sewing. "They built." A man covering himself. It looked like the wicker man on fire. You could see someone throwing a Molotov cocktail. "They soldiered the wires."

Some people even crawled; they stayed on their bellies crawling around for good. Careful not to be seen by the spotlights during the night hours. Everybody stayed down. "People stayed out of sight from the spotlights. Everybody listened to the rated R music without lyrics." The low-pitched music notes, when people were seen. "The notion of someone being seen hit a low note, like 'get down.'" There were musicians all over the abandoned city being informed on, because of behavior. The lights were all very bright. "And when people were seen, shots were fired. Everybody needed permission to enter certain areas." And everybody needed permission to enter inside. They went indoors when the light hit. "And again, people needed permission to enter indoors." And permission to get out. "Everybody had guns. When everybody saw shots were fired, they were all forced to check things out by one another." Everybody saw. "They took cover." Sanctity. Cover. "Zero Gs. Sleep. The vastness of space." Cradle your body by, "The vastness of space, the black ocean. Looking up."

They originated from the forest and built the land. The land. They took down the trees with the tools they had and sanded them down into nothing by use. Tools. By using their tools the right way, they sanded them into nothing. After they tore up the land, they were left with items like gunpowder and C4, weapons, tools, and gadgets. They built cocoons for themselves, a cradle intended for sleep. Hammocks. They put their bodies into machines and robots that dug into their joints and muscles to put them to bed, and put their minds to sleep by hooking them up into stasis, bone massaging machines, muscle massaging, you name it. "This is what dreams are made of. Stasis and war were a good couple when you wanted to relax."

They used technology like strip mining to attack others not obeying the law. Drift. Stasis. They drifted into stasis; they ravelled up the technology to make advanced weaponry. They turned off their tech, as it would have been in light of making things an extra step easier, harder. Sometimes they did not originate from the forest. "They used their supplies." They curled up. "They mastered time travel." They made their destinations the same weight as the past they wanted to live again. "And they used their town to prepare for stasis." Time travel. Fall out. They had to fry the land sometimes for extra parts, or even to make it to space, since flying there is incredibly dangerous. Technology. "Fallout." Fallout. The order for technology was endless in which to make. They had a multitude of machines that they put the wires together to soldier them, which made new ends and old hardware. "Soldiered, new tech, new hardware." Like they were restoring it. Some were asleep; they were simply hypnotized while walking around. They stayed on their bellies, crawling around out of the way of spotlights. "They stayed down, abandoned.

They were taught for survival." Music played 24/7 and only got louder when things started to happen, or people were getting close to restricted areas. "Even bullets whizzing past their heads, they continued to play. Shout into their instruments." When shots were fired, people were seen, which they compared to a viral outbreak, an infection. "Everything was guarded and powered by electricity and technology. By security, nothing they owned was safe, so they all hunkered down the cheapest way possible to refrain from the opposite of abandoned, fallout." They all stayed down by their mounds of cash, or groups of technology and present a way of life, for people in the village. "Of course, everybody counted on sights in the village." If it looked cheap, they kept it. "When quarantines lifted, they all showed off their weapons and traded in the dark. They placed their technology and talked about money." When the price was negotiated, they turned on the light real fast and everything disappeared, and everybody were gone. What happened next was unreal to them. I was thinking. "Thinking."

"Crystal." Crypt. Sight. "Money." They came in what's next.

Everybody stayed down. "They stayed down." They ducked, and someone said, "He showed me his blouse." The man flashed off his coat. He was showing off loaded with guns he intended to trade and sell.

They stayed down because there was war. In the back in the middle of war, they were trying the guns out in the directions they had fire to refrain from pointing at the wrong person's head. "When they learned greed was on the table, they turned to war and offered assistance to one another in the village." By doing this until all others were clean, they knew there would be war, which was the beginning of cloaking technology because they stayed clean, so clean that every sin was wiped off them until they were unnoticed, invisible. When everybody cleaned up, they wandered into war with an inconspicuous grin on their faces. They were gone like the wind.

"They scared people to death." To death without breathing or seeing things again.

There is war. "Everybody stayed inconspicuous like there was no war, pretending to pick up things and shop. When a would-be wanderer or wanderers came out, they blasted them in war for being involved or affiliated. Everybody was clean, and in this village, everyone knew the protocols; of course, they changed when people were blasted because all others knew. That and they knew all others knew; they spied to see if they were spied upon. That and they told others to go to refrain from being seen so that they could change after being seen. And when we shopped, they knew there were traitors in the city, so they all stayed undercover to watch what people were like abandoned.

War. "Stasis."

"Grievances." Stasis.

Soul. Food.

Grievances for the soul of minion. Grievances. "Grievances." Soul. "The soul. Soul of minion. The soul." A bomb went off. Grievance. "Bomb went off. War. Grievance." Grievance, a bomb went off. A bomb went off. "It went off."

Soul. At the heart of minion. Heart of minion. "They forgave themselves." They danced away. Danced away. "The soul of minion forgave himself, who then danced into the clouds." Away in the clouds. "Minions. Who forgave themselves, danced away forever. Forgave themselves. "They danced into the clouds." Forever. Wars. "Grievance. They danced away forever.

Grievances. "Grievances." The soul. "Soul. Why minion?" It's because minion is adept from evil. "The more evil a wanted man is, the greater the fame was." Infamy. Evil. "And so to it, the people who went missing were taken." And when gone for too long, they backtracked by remembering things. Then tracked. Tracked. Someone saw one following his memory. They tracked. He came from that way. "Backtracking, careful not to miss something." Miss. "Because. Adept. Is evil. The more evil, the more torture there would become." Infamy. A relic within, evil. "The most evil, tortured their victims with them." They took their victims with them. "And so to it people froze." They backtracked. "Tracked. Track." When they track. They backtrack. "Evil." People back tracked. "Tracked back."

Tribe. The tribal. "The tribal."

It missed. They went missing. "What missed? What missed. Who went missing?" What? "Backtracked? They missed." They missed. They backtracked.

They back tracked. "Track back. Backtracked."

Tracked back, the Halloween started like this.

"It was said war happens." War happens. "A bomb went off. A bomb went off." It was what I said. "When Halloween happened. It was said." War happens. Happens like this.

"A bomb went off." A bomb went off. "Post Espionage. It was said." Said.

They were tracked on down, "And everybody back tracked. They were back tracked everybody, tracked. If they noticed something weird, they tracked back." Back tracked and tracked back. Track. "Everybody tracked. They tracked back." Whenever they tracked, back. "They tracked back."

Track. "Tracks."

"The origin." Back.

Tracking started with a picture from the mind, a man drew. "If the picture I drew did this in my mind, then when I went, I would see if it were real." If it were real, I would no longer be imagining things. Lest I ever imagined things. They became rich.

If the picture I drew were like the map on the floor, then it was real, and the map is too. If it weren't real, the location in my head was real. If thought showed that it was there when I went, then the map was real. "The origins of the map." They took the picture out. "Picture out." He drew. "He drew."

The origin. Origin. "Origin."

Without it, there would be origin. "Origin. No origin."

"A long time ago there was peace. A long time ago." Between the interferences of eternity and now, there was peace, and before that, there was even more peace. "Even more peace. Because there" was nothing. Peace was there because people knew how to think. "They said," watching the crowd. "Let's see if they make it." Everyone was peaceful. The crowd dispersed into nothing; everyone evaporated. I ran some water. "I drank it up." There was peace. I drank the water up. Sundown, everyone was there because they were there to meet. "Once upon a time." The night went on. I interfered just walking by, like I was there to meet too. I was there to meet too. I shook hands. "I really didn't want to meet. I just wanted water." I thought that people had my attention, but it was not my attention people had. It was how I looked. I was never bothered, and by the end of the night, I only wanted water. I only needed water. "Water."

There was peace, time ago. There is peace time and time again. "They developed peace in their minds by doing it, which produced a subliminal message in their mind that portrayed something in reality. Then, sometimes, they went on to building it, which produced objectively permanent structures." This message they kept by taking the structures down. After living their fond memories. "Fond, fond memories. Let's see if they make it." I took a trip into exospace by letting my mind rest while a robot shook all the crevices of my bones and rattled me to sleep." When I was broadcasting, I started another machine to make it to the speed of light. "Radio waves are as fast as the speed of light. I took off into the future, and I flew through the net." I checked it out to see what they were up to. When I saw, it was so that they had all the documents. "They were there to meet. Once upon a time." The night was there, like flailing arms. I was there to meet myself. "I needed to meet." I needed water. They had not my intention, not my attention but my intention they had. "How I looked."

I was never bothered by the end of the night because I never bothered. I only wanted water. "Water." Water.

I was born, and years later I could speak and reason. I worked my arms out until they grew feathers, and eventually until they had enough lift to fly off the ground. "I was born to speak." I flailed my arms until they grew feathers, and I stuck to ground. I grew so tough that I lifted the earth off from its rotational axis into heaven with me.

Grievances. The soul of minion.

"Grievance." Minion, soul.

"Espionage." Espionage. Plate. "Splatter." Splatter.

"Grievances." Grievances. Espionage. "Espionage."

War never changes. When it does, people change, which changes war. "There is change in their background, no war. Just like as there was no war, just as there was no change." Change, war. People change; when they do, the weight of the planet should be changed too, for the sake of war, for our past, forgotten loved ones. Change." The shape of the planet war. "Future." Change.

"War." Espionage. Espionage.

"Everybody out!"

I took off after espionage. "Espionage."

"War." Espionage.

"I knew that I would run into trouble." And yet later, I'd run into trouble. "I run into trouble. Trouble. I'd run into trouble." Trouble.

"War." Espionage.

People run into trouble. "Run into trouble." When they run into trouble.

"Warp." Warped.

"It was." I took them all out on the computer by searching through viruses and neutralizing the threats. "I thought about them sitting on the computer looking for trouble, and I thought about happiness." When I neutralized them, I logged them off, and I woke up the rest of them by logging off. "Was." I took off to log them out. "I prayed happiness." When I neutralized them, I woke up those signed up, those in exospace. And the meanest and baddest one of them all knew I had skill. His skill was original. "So I hired him. Hired him."

"Behind enemy lines." Shoot.

"Everybody out!" The captain screamed.

"Everybody sits in their advanced technology and prepares for war." We see people are getting down for war. And we would go back to the old days, hand-starting fires. If that doesn't work, then they would sing to everyone they capture, putting them to sleep, access coms to exospace, then blow up the planet by cranking the music up so loud they heard their minds. "By cranking the music up so loud by sing, I meant." And play instruments until there is peace, such so that you can hear the mind from so much peace. "Peace." They prepared; in trenches they go. Everything down is idle, but on, "Down." Not in use. Sang. "Sing to the enemy so far that it blankets the land, a serenade of sleep."

'Very body out! "Everybody out."

"And if it kept, you would blow up the planet first, the one you stand on. Then wake up everyone from sleep, stasis, within technology, comas, etc. You would have to log everyone on the computer out then fry exospace through electromagnetic pulse." War is accomplished when we conquer war by changing the weight of the planet to a shape, one we're comfortable of. Then we change the shape of the planet we are, to change war. "The last time war happened, we conquered it." And the last time war conquered, we copied it. War conquers when you do it, not let war happen. "You made a sacrifice, blow up the planet and then the tech. If you did not wake everyone up, then people become lost, and others die, some go insane etc. So deactivate technology and then wake everybody up from with in their dreams." Press a button on their minds. Log them back in and set the electromagnetic pulse just right, on the floor. When we've conquered those techniques, we will change the shape of the planet, then the weight of it. Then we'll change. "War."

"Everybody out!" The man in charge yelled.

Signature,

"Doctor Pathic"

Signed,

"Scribbly line"

"Fifteen years into the future, nonstop computation and engineering. We changed!" The last time we computated fifteen years, there was war, because we missed espionage. "Missed espionage. Computer messages." Computer messages. We learned war was because of the weight of the planet, like someone pressing on your back, so we engineered it to change its shape. We lived everything in that shape and then changed it to match a certain weight. We learned the changes are for what was right, not for what was correct. Fifteen years later. "In reality, what they saw was not war but a theory. It was not logical enough for them to see. But logical enough for them to live." Logical enough for them to see. War, they thought, lived in their minds forever. They changed its shape, the planet, war, to a weight, not a shape, for sleep so that the mind sees the weight of war crushed. "The future, change." Robot. Last century, war, they missed something. They missed us. They changed the planet. "They changed the planet not to what was right but for what was correct. Fifteen years ago. Theoretics changed. Changed history. Changed history."

"Everybody out!" Everybody out! The man standing up in front of all echoes.

Espionage started. "The show was about to begin." Espionage was good enough for the mind to think about, because you would be condemned to learn why people were performing espionage. It's personal. "Their business is personal." Espionage can be fun too; just fill out the paperwork and read it.

The last time they saw was when treasure was shown in the tropics. "Shown in the tropics." They showed everything from dreams in picture form, to images that were once thought about in stories. "Their minds weren't aware enough except for the new lap record things, like a lot of money, the size of a house, certificates, and so forth." What I really knew was that I should claim it in the tropics. Because my idea led me out the door to claim all my money in the tropics because there were peace, not like in this war-stricken land, which is why I left. "Why I left. I was living in the tropics for some time now, and all I knew was to take the treasure in peace. From my currently discussed house, I walked to a clearing just near my house, like an offering, and saw that the microscopic evidence matched that of the evidence near my old house." I could tell because of what happened. Dirt moved. "I saw a strange marking in my mind on the site I just looked at. It showed coordinates to a location in my old house, but didn't say what."

I left for the past to my house to see if I noticed what the evidence suggested there. It should read something positive, like, "There is nothing there that was disturbed while I was out." But I was standing on the foot of a lot of microscopic evidence. But what really happened was when I checked the trap in my tropical house if anything was disturbed, I came to a conclusion that the spotters of this old house were interested in their traps from another place in time too, so they left this one. That and my evidence already suggested that the evidence from my current place struck me rich. The only way I could communicate was to follow old rules and prospect like I should be. I took a trip under my now new house, which was really just my old house because I returned. I moved to the tropics. It revealed a trap leading back to my old house, stating that some one knew of it or not, they discovered that it was just evidence, which was right because I just left from my old house into my new one at the time. There were signs like these where they were everywhere, and when everyone was in, I took my gold and left. "I even rented out houses in this trap gold-infested land. I looked back at my old house and needed to see who owned it." I left back to my old house in that rat and war infested house and realized that I needed the lease back. I broke in and stole the treasure microscopic or not after I got the lease back, but when I did get the lease back. That's what really happened. I realized that there was more treasure in the clearing just over there. I took it and realized that I came back to the house and it was a clown house, because I returned in war. In a war-stricken land I took the safest route to sell the house I returned. Clown house. War. Out. I was now rich from prospecting. I owned a clown house that I would soon turn into a maze and then a show after paying everything out.

"Treasure." Claim it now. "Claim it." The evidence of impedances matched up. I saw. "I left to my old home, stricken to war." The evidence suggested. Nothing here, it should read. "Disturbed." When I checked my old home, I had to check the trap to see if anything was there. My conclusion is that the traps were taken from spotters from a different time. I had seen communication from microscopy. Under my "New house." The microscopic evidence I discovered was just evidence. I "Took my gold and left." I rented houses. When I left my old house, because of war and a strange marking, I left back to my old house. I broke in and stole treasure. After I got the lease back. "Treasure in the clearing." The clown house in this war-infested land was there, because upon war's descent, the house was in the middle of war. Clown house.

I took the safest route there, took the gold, secretly I told, and took the house apart. For keeping. And left. In later days, it would serve as a fun house with a haunted past. War apartment. Espionage. "It." House.

Scribbly line,
Journal.

"Clown house." War apartment.

"Soul grievances." Soul grievances. About fifteen minutes. Soul, grievance, war. "Soul grievances." Still a generation. Hope. Picture. "War."

"War." Grievance. "Grievance." Soul. "Time limit ago, there were war." Espionage. "Grievance." Grievance. "Generation." Generation. "Hope. Pictures. War!" Espionage.

"War." Espionage.

Everybody out! The captain cluttered.

"A beautiful shadow." A bomb went off. "The smoke from the bomb covered the land, blanketing it and covering it." Dark night. "The nuke went off in a haze." Dusty fog covered it and blanketed the land. "Blanketed."

Everybody out! The Captain angered.

Doctor. "Doctor Pathic. Knots" Knots.

I thought. "I thought what I thought was treason." They thought they'd take their soul with them. I thought I'd take my soul with me. "Grievance. Take my soul and dream with it." Take my soul and dream with it. They idolize grievance. "Grievance for the old of minion. I take my soul and dream with it." For the. Grievance. "Minion. Take my soul and dream with it." A bomb set off. "Missed." Like always. "Grievance for the old of minion. Art. I lived in a room."

Doctor Pathic. "They were hiding a room." War. They were painting thought. I was painting by art with them. I was. They thought. "I said. I saw." I am. "Thought. Thoughts. Treason." They thought, die like a man, treason in thought. "Take," my soul with me. "Grievance." Take my soul. "Grievances." Soul minion. "Ask you favour? Jump." Take my soul. "Grievances." Old minion. "Take my, Soul." Bombs nearby. "It was time to go." Missed. Like always. The art of minion, grievance for my soul. "They idolize grievance, Grievances." The soul of minion.

"Living in a living room. Hiding. Art. Room." War. They were painting canvas, thought. "I was hiding by them." Grievance, "They said. I saw." I be. I am.

Doctor Pathic,
Signature
Scribbly line

Doctor narrating. "They said, narration."
He thought. "He was thinking." I was thinking. "He thought." I thought. I said. "He thought he had feelings." Feelings for whom, I saw. I had feelings for whom I saw. I was falling on a day like this. "I was falling beside the sun." Falling beside the sun. I had feelings for the sun. "For whom I had feelings for. Doctor Pathic. Dark sparkle." It looks like war but is there for Peace. "Dark sparkle. Imagination. Imagination." Dark sparkle.
Thoughts, I was thinking. "They were thinking. Thoughts, I said."

Doctor Pathic,
Signature
Scribbly line

When the time comes. I had feelings of imagination. For whom I saw.

Doctor Pathic,
Scribbly line

I was falling beside the sun. The feelings I had were of remorse, like having ashes from a cremation and throwing them into the lake of the sun. For who I had feelings for, "Doctor Pathic. Dark sparkle." Looking for feelings of peace. "Dark sparkle. Imagination."

"Dark Pathic."
Scribbly line
I forgave myself.
Dark sparkle. A war for the centre of the sun.

Doctor Pathic.

I was here to correct my words, interruptance. "Doctor Pathic." Correct my words. A moment. Interference. Crown on your head.

It fell on a day like this. They happen only every solar eclipse. "I saw dark sparkles. Dark sparkles." The planets realign every time of every period every nuclear winter. The planets are moving fast that they propagate through the universe and then back a billion miles a second. The thoughts I've had were worn into the mind I had. Every thought I had looped back to my previous one until I thought a new one. Like spending cash. "I said the words that wore in my life like a prayer." I saw my mind in the past. It wore in like an enchantment. Nuclear winter. "Not by the grievance of season." Nuclear winter is every vortex spiralling moment. I thought a moment, every vortex spiralling moment. I thought because it means something.

Falling. They happen every solar eclipse. Every solar eclipse. Dark sparkles. "The ocean of man."

Doctor Pathic.

I started out writing journals and made a heading.

Dark sparkles. "The ocean of man."
"Doctor Pathic."
Said.

War! On the morning of war. "They broke loose. They recorded their lives and put up a scare show." The war they fought, espionage. They let some in the scare house to top records. If they topped the records, they schooled espionage. Remember your past. "On the morning of war," I crashed. "Dark sparkles. They happen every realignment nuclear winter." The thoughts I had were worn into my mind. There was a machine in this room. A leather brain. This hall machine they used to make contact. They contacted only officials with it, and they used it in that room because that's where they moved it to. When they moved it there, they hooked it up to many other technologies. My thoughts were mixed. I spoke lines into my life, a prayer. "Doctor," Espionage. "Espionage." I witnessed great things. "My mind lived in the past."

There is a quasar whose energy is great. It looked like an asteroid, behemoth, its energies whose energies matched that of the quasar, who if they ever collided with earth, life started, would swipe the rock off the planet. Colonies started building off the planet into space, and when they got there, the planet would be wiped; they built into stasis, clean of life. The past was enchanted. There was an enchanted forest. Nuclear, this enchanted forest, winter, housed gold, "Housed gold." Because they saved winter, money seemed like it grew on trees. Grievance, of season. Vortex, moment. I thought. "Vortex." The last time nuclear winter, it switched on, and happened every vortex spiralling moment. I didn't need anything. Vortex. "Every vortex, spiralling moment."

I thought about it. "In the meantime, I will know."

Doctor Pathic,
Scribbly line

Then, Memory said. Once upon a time in a vortex. "Vortex."
Everybody out! "Everybody out."

"Fortune." Fortune. I wrote many journals, and they all pertained to originality. "Looks to us all." Looks to us all. Fortune. The last time things happened, they started with a bang. Then everything fell into stasis. The last time I seen, I saw. Fortune looks to us all.

Fortune is only when workers in a factory buy their own goods and use them on other workers. Like a fortune cookie. Your fortune would only be unless; the fortune cookie is made by others in the factory, the ones who print the notes.

"The fortune cookie's notes. The fortune cookie's lies."

In life, people die. Who dies? No one should die. They should work out until they become alien. The beginning of stasis is like the end. The beginning of stasis. It is like the end because everything puts you to sleep, and is as fast as a sleep is, like you don't want to wake up until the end.

"Sparkles." Sparkles. The stars shine "Dark sparkles." Every shining star.

He ran up the alley in backward seven. Nightfire. "The alley he ran up in a backward seven." Night fire.

He ran up the alley then tailed a building in a backward seven. He agent bullets and performed the correct manoeuvre. The manoeuvre left in a backward seven. The bullets tailed him and stopped when he darted right in line of a backward seven; the bullets chewed the building. The bullets danced his manoeuvre in an L from down going forth, a backward seven. The bullets danced. He dodged the bullets, dancing on his tail. I started a fire. Before any shooting, he ran to the right, away from the threat. He ran up the cement, Nightfire. I started a fire because of abandoned. He tailed three rounds going off.

"He ran up the alley in a backward seven." He performed the correct manoeuvres. One time, ago they said, we gotta go! "He tailed in a backward seven." One time ago, Nightfire. The next day. "We gotta go!" Nuclear winter. Night fire. It came from a long time ago. "He agent the bullets in the correct manoeuvre." The bullets hit but not him. "We gotta go!" I said; the bullets chewed the bullet proof vest I was wearing.

Doctor Pathic,
Scribbly line

"Once upon a time." He agent the bullets dancing on his tail. The bullets danced on his tail. Tailing him. The bullets danced on his tail. Away from the threat. Nightfire.

Nightfire. "He thought." He tailed the building again in a backward seven. Bullets hit but not him. The bullets hit. Night fire. Cement, in battle he thought. The bullets hit, Nightfire. He left a bomb there, thinking would give them a headache and cause manic depression, hopefully to get it done.

"Everybody out!" Captain screamed.

I thought.

Doctor Pathic,
Scribbly line

"Dark sparkle." They are the ones who happen every equinox. Dark sparkle. "Dark sparkles. Every equinox."

"Dark sparkle."

"Dark sparkles." Dark sparkles. "Sparkle. Equinox."

Dark, sparkles. "Sparkle darken."

In life people die. Who dies? In life, no one should die. "They should work out until they become alien." Sparkle darken.

Doctor Pathic,
Scribbly line

Sparkles. "Sparkling." Sparkly.

Nightfire, nightfires.
Doctor Pathic.

"Dark sparkle." Sparkle darkens. "Sparkle darken." "Dark sparkles."

Doctor Pathic,
Scribbly line

Dark sparkle. "It happens in the middle of earth." Sparkle darken. "Sparkle darken." Every middle earth. "It happened so quickly. The war, for the middle of earth. You threw someone in." You threw someone in. Saints be praised. "Be praised."

"Dark sparkle. Saints, praised."

A person tries to get some sleep, in line with sleeping perimeters, melatonin, REM, daydreams, then sleep. Sleeping man. "Sleeping parameters." Sleeping man. Sleeping man started at the middle of the forest. You could see a strange ghostly forest decorated fairy. There were subtitles below her. Subtitles. You could see peeking with one eye, and everything was upside down. Her face was upside down but looked like a decorated forested clothing fairy. She looked and went right side up.

He thought. "Sleeping man. He fell asleep."

"When they expect sleeping man, they expect a series." I thought, sleeping man. Sleeping parameters.

Doctor Pathic.

Sleeping man.

"The centre of the Earth is burning like the sun."

War happened near the middle of the Earth in dark fire, the middle of earth. "Happened in the middle of earth." Dark fire. Dark sparkle happens for the sun. Dark sparkle is heroism in a bomb. Dark sparkles. "The heroic war happened when war occurred for the centre of the sun." A war for the centre of the sun. They built the war by changing the shape of the planet. The past came with it. "Came with it."

"Dark fire." War. Falling into the sun. "Dark fire." Falling into the sun. Dark fire. Brass instruments lit up the sky even in the middle of war. "Brass instruments." In the middle of dark fire, brass instruments, the sky. The first minute, instrument struck, war.

Heroism in a bomb. "They went to war in the centre of the earth."

"Everybody out!" They said into the mic.

Heroic war. For the centre of the earth.

"Heroism. Earth."

Someone fell. It wasn't really someone falling. "It was the imagination of it. They were falling into a house, through the roof." You could not see the ceiling, but there was a hole in it, and not a real hole; it was a constructed opening that opens to the inside of a house, a set of stairs, and when they fell, you were not allowed to see the bottom because this being was not allowed to hit the bottom. It was like a play. "Like hell. But without the torture or hot fire." Torture or hot fire. The being, war, for the centre of earth. It's like hell. This being was there to fall, but not to experience hell." To show us what falling is like. Falling is like hell without torture. "And the fear from falling was there not to be experienced, but read." Falling. Fear was there to sit beside us, to read the story with us, from looking at the same book you are looking at, all while the narrator is narrating the same book with another just like it. You are sitting beside fear and you are not afraid of him reading from your book to your right over your shoulder. "You are afraid of what the book says to you because to you, from your set of eyes, you are afraid of the story."

You are also afraid of what everything looks like from your imagination while reading the story. Fear is reading a story, and it is the same story you are reading. He means to read the same thing you are reading. The story means something creepy. That you are following along while this story is going on. Eyes. My professor is reading a story while me and fear are reading along with him. "My professor is glancing back and forth from the book to looking at fear." He didn't even need to look at his copy of the book to read because fear was there. "Just looking at him was good enough to read a book." My professor is reading the same book as me and fear. I don't think fear was there to read a book; he was there for the fact that I was reading a book. Fear was reading a book. "I finished reading a book and so did fear." Fear finished reading the book. I finished reading the book. "Fear took off."

"Someone falling." It wasn't really someone falling. "They started out in mid air and then went through the roof, a hole in it, falling into a hole." After fear.

"Everybody out!"

Metaphorically.

"Two thousand years ago, I was calm and felt like reading."

"Reading."

They were reading the same book as me. They were reading off of fear like my professor did, read off fear. Fear is powerful. Metaphorically, I was reading. "I felt like reading." Reading. It looks like it just happened. Like two thousand years ago was on a pause screen and just happened. These words formed thousands of years ago into now. Just happened. Like this pause screen governed my feelings for reading. I was sitting down and was reading the present day, from thousands of years ago. "Thousands of years ago I read their present day." Present day. My thoughts with fear. My thoughts were focused on reading and changed from what I was reading to what I was looking at. "And what I was looking at was what I was reading." My thoughts changed from what I was looking at to what I was reading. Thousands of years ago. It happened two thousand years ago. These events never took place.

Two thousand years ago.

They started talking and said, "I am with you."

I am with you because "I am there."

Doctor Pathic.

"I was there because I saw an outlook." Was there. I was there.

I was there because I saw. "I am there. I see." I was there. "I was seeing." It started when I was there. I was there.

"Everybody out!"

I got out because I was there. I was getting out. I was seeing. When I was seeing, I was there. I saw. "I saw."

"Everybody out!" Everybody out!

One time ago there was a past. "There was a past." This past was so full it had to be the future because I could see it, and it may not have been my future but it exists as an alternate reality for someone's future. "Even then if I looked away, I would have thought about it like getting ready to see another reality." The future, I would have seen the future and experienced it, if that reality was mine, and so to it, is my future, if it is my future. Because I could think about it metaphysically, and thought about it, where it passed my thoughts it would be my future. My future.

The future.

The sky went dim. A bomb darkened the sky. The cloud from the bomb was like it, engulfed the sun. A corona gas cloud. It was like the bomb was the skies future. But the sky was tough; it could withstand one nuclear blast. The bomb was not my future because it didn't hit me. It was in the future, though, because I saw it. That was someone's future, over there. The bomb. It had to be the future, but not my future.

"Everybody out!"

An explosion. "Things come."

"Everybody out!"

A dark, black plague. "Bomb." A nuke. One where they plague, explosives.

"Everybody out!"

I set a bomb off.

"Set a bomb off." I set a bomb off. Bomb off. All those bombs were tiny. "Tiny. So I set a bomb off." I blew up the planet. Those bombs were tiny.

The bomb set off in the distance. "Someone's fame was in, wishing for war. Enchanted. They got what they had hoped they wished for. A bomb set off in the distance." In the distance.

"Bomb."

A bomb set off in the distance.

"Everybody out!"

Dark mist.

Beings from space, see the future that looks like a dark sky. It tells of omens. "People were watching." Again, that wasn't necessarily their future. They watch the sky for visions. You are allowed to dream about the future.

Dark omens.

"Everybody out!" Everybody out.

Black mist shows the sky like a poem in the distance. "Poetry in the distance."

"The skies slowly clear."

Everybody out!

"Omens."

"Future."

"Future apocalypse." Future, apocalypse. It started out with a gun, and he didn't finish the deed. He left from out of my sight I could see. He thought, "There's diner right there." I left.

"Everybody out!"

Another bomb set off. "I'm glad I wasn't there for the blast." There was a darkened sky.

"Black sky." Dark harvest.

I went to a park. It was nighttime, and I saw a hill. It was frosted. There were hills everywhere, and one so heavy behind me that I was forbidden to cross because it would have ruined the look of the park. My skin could have torn if I turned back. The music sounded like a rated R movie; it was deep and dark. Music sounding like after you murdered someone and are about to be scared to death in a park. Kind of like a theme park cast of music. The sky was black. There was a spotlight shining over the hill into your eyes. It was funny because this light actually looked like it lit up your vision to night vision. The frost stayed on your face but wasn't cold. You could stay out there for hours. I wanted to stay there forever, but I was prompted to go. Music at a night sky. It was beautiful.

A nuke went off. Standing far enough you could see your apparition. And luckily, not your apparition in the halo, engulfed in and by foggy, black smoke.

I set another bomb off. This night sky was like heaven stationed in hell, there to sit forever. This bomb I set off, it lit up everything I knew, the space behind me.

Fog. You know what fog is and not smoke.

It looks like a dark rainbow because of darkening mist engulfing the sun in the sky and the sun shining behind the fog. The darkening mist looks like a feeling, a dark rainbow. Like an evil scale of black to then forever eternal in hell, to evil. It looked like a dark rainbow to fog, then mist, then a shadow, then evil, up to forever, then eternal, stopping at hell.

"Stopping at hell."

"What puzzle." Misty summons.

A bomb went off.

I set another one off. "Another one off." And this time it was the place I loved. "Exospace." This time you could feel the radiation from my UFO. Simulating the death from a bomb, like that it was. It was in my UFO because if what I blew up, my home. You could feel it because the sensors were connected to everything this bomb was wired to, my home and furthermore the ship was born connected to that exospace, and you could feel the radiation from the reactor in my UFO. It was connected, and if it weren't, I would have felt the burn coming from off the radiation in reality, burning through me. Burn through me.

Everybody out! "Everybody."

"It has misty dark skies. A bomb set off because of people wishing. The park was my exodus. Misty, dark skies conjuring." I left to the park because I could see it. The park was dark, with green frosted grass. They tell because they expect the stories to stay fake. "They publish omens to tell the future for those that need it." Or you could take these readings and let them get to you. "Let them all come true." But it wasn't true enough the reading of this passage. "It already came true. They were publishing omens because you read the writing." It was already true, because it was written.

The truth was already written.

Dark, black, exodus, the park was frosted because it is like a past memory being outside playing with the snow, playing in the snow without a care in the world, but in a theme park in the night sky. You let snow go, fly up in the air looking up at it with a smile on your face. The theme park would be dark, like experiencing winter at night on the northern face of a planet; it got dark fast and still would be the day according to the hours. It never struck midnight yet. You knew it was night time when you've lived in the northern face of a planet. The park was like riding a ride you've never ridden before, like being blindfolded, and when you started the ride, you ripped off the blindfold to meet your maker. A dark black sky. This park is like riding in a theme park the first time. A mist darkens; it was cool. Then you wanted to see more, the smoke ring after another, riding in horror; bomb goes off, blanketing an already dead sky, but never hits you in your imagination because you couldn't see.

The stars flicker. So you left. Like a stunt. You wanted more. This time. The feeling is like ripping something off your skin after a while for the first time and feeling the soothe on top of your skin after a while. You left for the hills. You wanted to see if the frost is as friendly as you thought it was. You looked up and saw the ceiling of the sky. The stars were like no ceiling existed. The black sky was darkened like the ceiling. Black sky. A black mist, everything darkens like the black of space. Like wiping soot off on space seeing this space, chimney of black soot looking up into the darkness, seeing stars, this chimney black soot on space, a rock chimney held together by concrete, a transparent rock chimney darkens and you go inside without being told to go inside. Telling, the park looks like frost. The frosted grass. The clear hills. You kept going and saw more park. A mini loop and a lonely rider. The skies are clear.

Everybody out!

A bomb went off.

"Everybody out!"

This bomb was a story, much like priming a bomb.

Everybody out.

Dark sky. "The sky darkens." The park is like having a gun licence; it is reassuring to know that a park is there for you. It is like having a lot of food to take care of yourself. And you wouldn't give it up for all money in the world. The park makes you feel happy. The park is reassuring because if you said one word to all the people in the park, something would happen. "An apparition scribbles." Having food is like living in a park; that's all you need, "onto the forest clinging onto the mist." I took cover because the blasts were finally big enough. I had been watching, and I wouldn't pay for tiny bombs like that. This mist, a smoky ring. "We invited them because the blasts were big enough." They knew how to craft a bomb. They were now rich.

'Very body out.

Bombs.

"'ery body out."

"A bomb detonation means run! This looks like war, the mist." The park is very reassuring, "They can detonate as many bombs they like." The next dimension calls you. I let all those bombs go off because they were big. I secretly developed a nuke in my lab, like the ones they were letting off, because I am a fan, me and others invited them in.

"Everybody out!"

"This mist looks like war." The park is reassuring; the bombs go off in the distance. "They felt like they had run a million miles." A bomb went off. I countered that bomb with back fire. "They stood on the forest floor looking up. So many detonations have gone off; they show a tree glowing from a halo placed behind a black-eyed being, grey-skinned." It was time to go. "The tree was there because of detonations, the story." A tree grew in the mist of bombs being detonated. "A grey-skinned being watches." They took the land with them, and even the people who were bombing in. They accepted.

Many come back to the story of destruction. I watched some leave and, just like that, others had arrived. They said these halos were like stories to them; they left, and when they did, the premonition started over. I recorded this, "And one man said!" Grey knew that and was already gone with the people from the forest. They had enough technology to strip the land of its former shape and weight. So much weight that it forced a start over to happen, so let's make it good, or they face and witness, death faced upon death. And if that, life, rebirth faced upon death upon death. And more.

A man standing on a hill, the night lit hill. His apparition showing his salute. "Everybody out!" He screamed. That even his own shadow jumped at the might of him screaming.

"The being said," we need to take apart the land and make technology with it. If we take the land apart, we can make many strains of gunpowder. We crush up the land and make this gunpowder. Then below up the next heaviest thing, a rock, then paste, until it turns into a cutter. Then we cut things with the cutter until the land boils. Then we boil to dissolve the cutter into nothing to restore order, light.

Premonitions started. The way grey explained things was easy to understand. Someone starting war. Glad they were premonitions, and we could just walk away instead, watching them come true. Premonitions. But not for them.

"Everybody out!"

"War. Nukes. Nuclear spring." It was cool outside, too cool. I would freeze in one second.

'Very body out.

He saw them because of premonitions. Visions of lonely kids depressing out. This god-forsaken, war-stricken land.

Rich kids with nothing to do. Before they were trained or broken. Throw them around once and watch them lash out, until they saw your face, you salute.

"The season." The ballad of the wind.

'Very body out!

Ballad of the wind.

"They brought another bomb. I continued my prospection." I can. "'Verybody out!" I read, interrupted again this time with another nuclear threat. I pulled out a nuke faster than them. And set it on the table for them to have. They threw it out the door, and it flew right into space, and back to deep space, then up into exospace, then it blinked in the clouds. He stopped bombing. "Where was I?" The feel of the word is like, "Everybody out!"

It is like I was interrupted by war again. "Where was I again?" Oh yeah. "I was at war." A smooth significance. I can use any word and tell of significance like this. "I pulled another gun faster than him." Fire to the limbs is like a pinch. That would be good enough for, "War, interruptance." For connotation, but this time as an innocent connotation, the sky was smooth. And we gave up money for times concern without any shots, he agreed.

The sky.

"Everybody out!"

The bomb is smooth to the touch but not to the eyes. Any radioactive bomb is like wildfire to the skin, "Gaseous intent." They set off so many bombs they hooked into a star. Bomb, the destruction between differences is like a bomb. "Bomb." Destruction. Looks like a bomb going off, but the after shock. Bomb going off. You'd look to the sky. Destruction. A connotation for explosion, post, or pre app. Previous, destruction, bomb, explosion boom. Connotation looks like, "Gaseous intent." Halo is as is because halo is the persona of a perfect but deadly war. You saw the correct man's blood fly; he was holding a gun upon resuscitation but never fired. We had to be sure, so we let him die before disarming him and bringing him back to life.

Gunsmoke.

I juggled the gun in my hand, swapping it to the other hand.

Everybody out!

Gun smoke.

An explosion. When that bomb went off, we rewound time by taking pictures and videos to recast this explosion, but it hit nothing.

Gun fire.

Gun smoke.

Once upon a time a bomb went off.

Boom.

Upon one time. "War struck." The man said, "What? He hung up the phone."

A repair man was working on a phone line. He received a phone call from the repair line and the dialect was in Old English; it spoke, with breath, sounded like he ran out of breath. Images. Smoke ring. "Gun smoke."

Repair line, a man hanging on a line repairing it from a space station, touching down onto the planet. Being on that repair line is like hanging out of a space station, working on a repair line. The cables were metres in diameter. You could smell a breath of fresh air, and being on the line was like being in a vehicle hovering, lowered in the atmosphere many hundreds of feet in the air with no breeze.

"A bomb struck." Then one more bomb went off. Zero hour. I looked for cover after I was finished. I took my time. That bomb went off and quickly took a bite of the land. The breath was radiation. I scorched as many trees and dirt as I could. It blew up quickly as the land melted. I took cover at once as I did. "Once upon a time." A bomb. "Struck." A bomb. Gun. It struck because there was war. A dark, gaseous war. Cogs. Survival. Bombs. Those were the shape of war. I counteracted the radiation cloud by tearing up the land. When I tore up the land, I shot into the cloud many times, walking toward it until I noticed a cutter being formed by radiation frying my gun after looking for a loose mixture that would explode with the radiation of the cloud.

There was war.

"When there is war."

An apocalyptic explosion. These bodies were found alongside technology. "If I found war."

They were playing a play. Kids surrounded centre stage, and when the music started, they all rushed away from the centre of their circle. The play was over. The kids' performance was like smoke blowing out from under everything. They picked up from the blast, and before they hit the ground, it was over. We thought we were in a play but only imagined the play in a spectacular performance we thought we were in. The play.

They thought about a bomb going off. They were narrating, a shadow. One antagonist is playing the apparition on this side, in the shadow of war. And on the other side in the shadow of war, one was playing with a puppet. "Nuke." I was allowed to get away, get away with the story. "I got away with the story beside my life." I took out everything I owned. "I made a picture." I made a picture. A bomb went off. "I noticed." A space station was in sight of repair. "Why certain bombs went off. Bombs went off. The reason bombs went off was because of the technology we had. We let these bombs go off."

The bombs were so big they obliterated all of space, and even the Big Bang; that is why we let them off. That and when encountered by our reality, we had black holes of power. But that was not all; we took cover in the crevice of space, in a canyon that wasn't real. How? We programmed computers to see what we wanted as not real. The numbers were right. We let those bombs go off. In the beginning. In this picture I wanted my thoughts. I was happy I could finally talk inside my head that on all what was going on. I wanted them to think. I wanted them to think mental suggestion, because of what I did.

The shadow, "Primitive life," was showing bombs going off. The shadow of an individual. "I thought, curly haired individual, who looked like it was from hell; he wore a tiki mask, red, and had black cardboard straw hair, stapled hair, with its tongue curled, looking up at the sky. I thought. The being looked right at me with its right eye, like this man's tiki mask was looking at me. The feelings this being had were of laughter, but only while it was looking at me, like a being not of this world. What was really not of this world was what it said. After all, it was a shadow. When I acted what this shadow said, I saw, and when I saw, I felt feelings of laughter like this being once thought about, like this being once did. I thought about mysterious things, like narrators, personas, antagonists, and thought about feelings of what people said. The shadow was gone, and this being must have felt feelings of disclosure. Full disclosure. Because the being left from thought, not by action.

I thought about feelings people were thinking. I watched the news, read books, and thought about why people acted that way. "I thought," the tiki man, "It must have been interesting they were doing that, and if it weren't, then I'd have to pull someone over and book them, and if they didn't tell me what they thought." That must have been how they were feeling,

"The tiki man thought," and if it wasn't, then I would be out of there to let them leave. And if they didn't leave, I'd let them go. I felt like nervousness, and what, "The tiki man said," I saw was a man in the moonlit dusk, "Transparent chimney," except there was no moon. There was a pale blue sky with around fifteen hundred trees apparition in the background, dawn; after the hour of midnight and witching hour, I saw dawn. The man was standing in the middle, faced away from the trees. He was slightly to the left of the middle. He was feeling like a newcomer. He also felt like waving with his right hand. He felt that way because he was not a newcomer; he was there to tell me how I feel. He left in a hurry after he told. I noticed that this war was only in my feelings. What was left was the shadow of dark, holes in a smoking land.

In a smoking land because of friendly fire. I'm glad they only fired at their direction and not at them.

I felt like the dusk. The feeling you feel. The feeling you feel after Christmas day. It was to tell me something. From the beginning. I saw a being leave. He was dead. "Or so I thought." It was to tell me, being leave, how he feels. Far cry. One tells you what he saw; he felt like one who made everything while I saw someone on the other side of him. I felt like everything. And saw no one. I said, "I felt like it." I saw a man again, and this time he asked me a question. He saw me, saw me and thought and thought he might leave. I asked, "What makes you want to leave?" He said, "I saw." Right after he said, I saw. "He saw." He saw.

Afterwards, I saw, and left. I felt new. I felt happy.

The next day. "I felt like leaving." I saw. I felt like leaving.

Somewhere else in the universe. "I felt like leaving; someone was actually leaving." One heading, "Leaving, I'll tell you what, I am leaving." Out the door was a sign that someone who rushed out, died. I needed to be there for the multiverse theory, so I left but I didn't die. I thought about leaving. I then said telepathically to this being that just left, "Does anything happen if I leave too?" He said, "Do you feel like leaving?" He said philosophically, I woke up from a dream. Telepathy.

Next year, "I thought. I felt like leaving." I felt this way because I saw. I felt like, "Leaving, it's me. I'll tell you what, I'm leaving." I had witnessed a suicide. What really had happened is I left because of all that I learned from the media. The media and friends sucked. So I left after what I had learned."

"I'm leaving." I noticed people were there. "I'm leaving." And instead of thinking about where to go, I thought about where I felt like going, and when I'd seen, I thought I witnessed feelings of remorse, and it was so because people built a temple and did not feel like entering it or living with it. The way people act in society today are that they live in buildings they build. I found some in a park. I thought about my past. "My past."

I knew that if I thought about feelings, I would see. These feelings weren't, these feelings weren't really feelings, it was a conversation. My thoughts started acting as though I was there. Where I were was with was with no one. "I wasn't there."

My first moments of kinesis.

"They were there too."

"Everybody out."

People were there, Molotov Cocktails, I thought about what I felt. I felt like an invisible antagonist, not an invisible man. Molotov cocktails. Invisible man I thought about living with them. I only wanted to see "Molotov cocktails," how they acted so I could get the right thoughts and leave. If I did "Molotov cocktails," then my thoughts were right. I should be able to travel all places I thought about from that event to get whatever it suggested. Molotov cocktail goes right over my head. If it didn't happen that way, it suggests a setup theoretically, technically. If I wasn't, "These molotov cocktails, these Molotov cocktails," allowed to think right, like someone was commanding me, there would be war. And again, none of this actually happened; they were only just thoughts.

A bomb went off.

"Bomb."

Suggestion feels that way because I feel that way. "Feels that way because."

When suggestion feels that way, you feel that way too. I saw a man was looking.

When treason is real. There was treason. When war is real, there was war. This means war. "This means war!"

A, "Look out."

The picture looks of imagination. "Looks of Imagination."

"Sparkle."

Sparkles.

Sparkling.

Sparkle, happen.

The picture looks of imagination. "Looks of imagination."

Sparkling.

"There was war." There was war. Then I remembered how to say it. I said, "There is war!"

Sparkle.

"Does sparkle happen?" Does sparkle happen. Contact happens when sparkle happens. You make it. Make it, as in, arrive to, not by engineering. You'd use engineering to make contact only when they were ready to clear out. If you made engineering, you would have made a way to one, depending on if you made the engineering. The engineering opens up for use. "Engineering made it possible for a certain way of life. People arrived first inside for engineering. It opened up for contact. It welcomed people for prosperity, and the news was on."

"On the front-page news,"

There is war.

War!

When writing time stops, you can record anything you want. When you are done, "publish it," publish it. So you can do it.

Like a time, "Sprinkling," sprinkling stops.

They look like explosions.

They look of imagination, because of imagination.

"Stars sparkle." Sparkle.

"Do common questions come to the fair?" What does gypsy do? "Do stars sparkle?" Does gypsy have an imagination? "Do sparkle have an imagination? Sparkle. The picture looks of imagination. Picture looks of imagination. After stars sparkle. Once stars sparkle. Does sparkle have an imagination? Stars sparkle." Does a star sparkle? "Stars sparkle?" If stars spark. Stars sparkle. If stars spark. "Sparkle. Sparkling." Stars are sparkling. "Which one is sparkling? Which one? Stars." Stars. "A blast means nothing to sun." The sun would think. "A Sparkle." Is this one sparkling? Stars sparkling. "Sparkle. Stars sparkle." How much stars are sparkling? "Sparkle." Sparkling. "Sparkling." Which one is sparkling? "Which one?" Are stars sparkling? "Stars sparkle because stars sparkle." Which one? "Does a star sparkle?" Stars sparkling. "Stars sparkling." Which stars are, "Molotov Cocktail." sparkling? Sparkly. "Sparkle. Do stars sparkle?" Stars are sparkling. Stars sparkle. "Sparkly. Do you have an imagination?" Imagination is why stars sparkle, in the sky. "They sparkle because of imagination." They sparkle because of imagination. "Sparkle because of imagination. Sparkle because of imagination." Fifty bucks you can't make it, "Stars sparkle in the sky." They sparkle because of imagination. "If stars sparkle." Do they skarple? "Stars sparkle." Skarple. Skarple. Sparkling. "Imagination looks like this." Sparkle. Stars, "Sparkle. Imagination is when." Stars skarple.

Math sparkle, because of stars, or?

Does math solve stars?

"Sparkle."

Sparkle, "Because of math?"

The sky, "Sparkle because of stars?"

Because of the sparkling sky, "Stars sparkle."

In the sky, spars skarple.

Stars sparkle in the sky.

"Stars have sparkled in the sky because of imagination." The picture looks of imagination.

Because of imagination, stars sparkle in the sky.

The sparkle sky.

It looks of, "Rotten scoundrel, he made it!" imagination because of stars sparkling in the sky.

Imagination.

"Imagination," Imagination, is why stars sparkle in the sky.

Sustenance.

Sparkle.

Today, "Remote."

"Spy."

Remote.

"Detonation."

"Scarab beetle!" I called for him. "Scarab beetle!" He came running after me when I shouted his name. "Scarab beetle is his name." That's what I called him because he was a scarab beetle. "Scarab beetle!"

"Remote location," remote control. "I felt like I was bleeding. Like I had a wet dream in my mind, which came true, full of blood. Like there was an apple balancing on my skin, on the right side of my head while I tasted blood in my mouth. I felt it, like skin on skin." I saw a man I was spying on, and he came out of a drycleaners frontal store. I thought about getting his attention. I was told to spy on him. "I felt like spying on him because of my feelings." I felt like spying on him was the way. I had feelings. I had thoughts, "Thoughts," in my mind. I thought about what I was thinking and it was, abnormality, like I belong in a freak show. I was thinking about it.

The things "My boss said were always weird." What my boss said was, "I thought about a man coming out of a drycleaner's. Spy on him and confirm my feelings of happiness." This man. He wasn't really coming out of a drycleaner's store. He went "In," and the suit wasn't really a suit. "It was an invitation to investigate the dry cleaning." I investigated this man's posture and got a glimpse at nothing. I tailed him to what might have been his house, and when I got there I saw something strange. "I saw the man leave his house when he got there," a man looked like an unimpressed doctor warning someone. He walked through the front door; the suit he was carrying disappeared instantaneously. I went back to the drycleaner's, and the man with the suit walked back in. I was tailing him. "I thought I was seeing things, but what really happened was that I had a mental condition. And the man with the suit wasn't really a man with a suit. The suit was there to signify the condition I had. When I found out the suit wasn't front store analogy, I picked up the suit and ditched."

The man who came out of a drycleaner's store.

Stars sparkle. "Stars sparkle."

"I was doing something. I thought about it." I felt like doing something. "I felt like thinking. I felt like thinking about moments of life." Moments of childbirth. Monumental awareness. I felt like thinking.

Monumental awareness. Doctor Pathic.

"Everybody out!"

Awareness.

"I was doing blood work in a lab. Then another sample came in." And boom, on the door someone rambled. Bang, someone was there.

"Monumental awareness."

Everybody out!

"The type of blood, is the type of blood." To use type of blood twice in a sentence attracts the article a tent, because once is to think about it, and the other is to do it. Theoretically, metaphorically. Saying anything more than once means something, just like good old-fashioned alliteration. It's said an EMB, Electro-Magnetic-Bomb, went off." Just an explosion going off, would. Once, for the sake of study and when mentioned more than once, gives rise to an article. This means that the article has reason and definition. "To say it is really a scholar's way out." They say it, "And mean it's a subject to say it more than once." And retromortis is a certain type of blood from a corpse after it has died, a corpse. A man pushing on a corpse's shoulder. "It leaks molecules." Retromortis is a stimulant that exists in the blood. "Retromortis exists in the blood because of molecules seen seeping through other molecules located close to the skin and within the skin." An earlier study states what pathogens are there for. Pathogens exist in the air because pathogens were created from a lab. "It was created in a lab because if it weren't, then people would die from real pathogens, carried by the skin and other afformaties. Pathogens are made for and from bacteria." That is why pathogens were created in a lab. "This states that in a lab, there would be no problems the pathogen could see, so it would be able to be flown through the planets and etc. Like an alien landing on this planet. Pathogenical, is pathogenical because of time." It states that pathogenical, exists, because you won't go easy on reality. This means that pathogenical is there to slim down your reality and give you a break without killing you. Using shortcuts, taking chances, and etc. "They had too work under harsh conditions because of the war." Once all the bombs went off for that day, the blood work should have been done, or else risk death.

They came in. "Monumental, awareness."

Is "There a coffin here?" The coffin looks like an elongated hexagonal figure, oblique, chiral. "The outside is black, including the lid." The coffin took cover. A mysterious thought seeped into my mind. "The coffin opened up and put one to sleep." That was the thought that entered my mind and when the blast went off. I remember. "One layer down is metallic paint colour on the collar of the inside of the coffin." One layer inside of the coffin is fabric and is plain white. The coffin opened up. Inside the coffin is a body. I remember. Sitting on and stapled up behind the half-open coffin is red fabric, just like Dracula's coffin red. When you notice the coffin, only when you notice it, both doors to the coffin were open. Only if you notice it. "What you saw is red fabric, like Dracula's coffin satire. Except it is not silk like Dracula's coffin, looked similar to it is satire."

The coffin is there for decoration, and so is the red fabric. It looks good enough to decorate the story. "The coffin is coloured black because it was at a funeral."

The coffin is usually sealed shut, "Sealed shut," inside a crypt beneath the streets, though. "This is a special day. Dracula's body will now lie there, in the picture of this cascade to show how important the remains are." Important the remains are. The coffin separates the mummy; the crypt is located in and below the graveyard. "The antechamber is above a mummy. The mummy separates the ritual chamber and the antechamber. The mummy separates the antechamber and a crypt. A graveyard is located above a crypt." Tombs are located beside a sarcophagus inside a grave. A sarcophagus is separated by the ritual chamber, and the ritual chamber by a sarcophagus. If this is true, the sarcophagus is in the tomb. I went down like hell to get the treasure.

Everybody out!

"The imagination was there." The right imagination.

The body bag contained a mummy.

Mummy.

Sarcophagus.

Crypt.

A mummy is lying inside the sarcophagus.

Crypt.

A tomb is in the sarcophagus beside a coffin.

The mummy is inside the coffin, beneath the graveyard above a crypt.

The coffin is with the mummy inside the crypt.

Coffin.

The crypt is open beside the graveyard.

Coffin.

Crypt.

Coffin.

Coffin.

Coffin.

Crypt.

I got up after rest.

They played, and it wasn't instruments. "Play sleeping man today."

They were mystical. "Mystical. Come in." What is that?!? There was a light there. You saw it. "I walked past a light. The picture looks of imagination. I saw a light." When I saw a light, I had already walked past a light. Walk past a light. "I walked past you too. I caught up to you, "Then walked past the light. The light flickered." Light flickered. It was because I walked past you too. "I saw in the maze. I followed you in." The maze, "I followed you in. Walking behind you. I walked past you. You were walking past the light. The maze looks like dust settled, on the ground, before two red panels, soft to the being's touch, gritty to mazes. A haze coloured the room with dust there. I walked past you."

Missed, the dust settled in the haze, because I walked past there. It never got to me, "And may not have got you either. I walked further into." I walked past you. "The maze and the bordered boundary surrounded me. I saw you back there. But not after I walked in." I saw you surrounding the maze, but not from my point of view. You told me" I was there. "But I saw you at the entrance. I saw you enter, the entrance, to the maze. If you were right behind me, I'd think about you standing there." You weren't there. "You were in the maze with me. I walked past you, in the maze just now.

Enchanted Forest.

Hymns. "Enchanted, hymns."

"The picture looks of imagination."

A man before a forest. I saw it. "I saw what I was looking for. It was a good idea." One came in, and I said, "That's a nice shirt." I idoled with the idea. I ate the ideas that one was carrying. They looked like ideas. "They tasted like them too." I was with a set of eyes, and my legs walked to scare people so that I may get peace. "Others I heard, fought with their arms and legs. I scared people for peace and ate ideas for food. Walking Enchanted Stallchild.

Stallchild.

I saw snow. I was standing on top of a hill. "It was day and it was cloudy." Hazy clouds. They were calm and straight, across the sky. "It was like if I went to the top of those clouds, I'd keep going from seeing the top never ending. The top of a building."

"Sparkle. It was in my imagination." Sparkle.

I heard something. It was when I came out. I noticed because I was too involved in my doings, afterwards. "I heard something from behind. I heard an eerie whistling. I was standing in the hall and remembered that whistling from the past from another life, the whistling stood behind me." I remembered what whistling was. I remembered whistling, "I remembered another life." I learned how to whistle again, from another life.

Espionage.

When espionage starts, it's time to go. "There is war!" Amongst the greatest in the universe, war happens. "Just like that, war can be over if it weren't for conjunctions with the mind and imagination, for behaviour what reality offers for you. Espionage, because there is trouble. And another, because you stole and were caught." There are two ways that can happen. One, you were in the middle of a thriving society and stole, and someone became self aware by counting their stacks, letting you out the door in the middle of tax season. And the other, because you stole and did it in the name of murder, without all the ethics like taxes, GST and PST will save you from, and like a bank, or interest, or commodity or a mortgage, school or university, or anything like that comes with a statement that you would die.

"In reality, there is another way of doing things. You can either vote to become anonymous in society and then steal everything at the top or height of your career. Or you can start war and kill everyone then take everything. This should happen when certain things don't add up, though. Certain things like when your mortgage fails, school turns you down for failure, you quit your job for many reasons, you can't pay your taxes, and all of the above simultaneously. This states that there is conspiracy, and some people don't get upset to what they need with life alone, so they kill everyone. I was thinking about everything, steal it at the height of my career like I've seen what most rich people do.

Espionage. "War!"

"Everybody out!"

Hooked up. "There is a TV there. I turned it on, and basic white noise was playing. I went to sleep just before this. My mom said work out a lot and get plenty of rest. I followed her instructions, and I was so built that it made me alien with far greater intelligence and a lot better nerves for telling people." I messed with the TV, and when I did, it turned off. Everything went online, and the TV went off, idle, Down. "It was replaced with all new wiring, and the power light was replaced with a neon red light. I thought about this TV's engineering." I thought, this TV, in my passion, I would fix the TV. I was hooked up.

Everybody out.

Everybody out.

"I was given too many good ideas. Like when there was a mental suggestion there and when you had money to do something and your parents drove to your favourite store. And if something important comes up the week after and you spend all your money. That too many good ideas." If they gave me the correct ideas and made it happen for me, these correct ideas would have turned me into a scientist. It would have turned me into a scientist. With all the correct ideas. She wanted to say something else, but she said. It sounded like this, she said, "Honey, I left money on the counter for you." On the counter for you. She was in disguise but not so that she could be seen; the disguise covered her up and the clothing was dyed a certain colour so that she could be seen, like being on a painted background would cover you up, and the next second you could see into their eyes, that close and that disguised. Under disguise.

"I took the money and counted it there, and I left." Left. When I left, I bought something, and only when I had no more money. I was then picked up by my mom after calling her. I was surrounded by life such so that I had terrible ideas about what to do if I ever came into contact with another. These thoughts always led back to me getting beat up, but ever happened. I waited because I was not allowed to get in their bubble. "We left, and I had wished I had looked away." When I fell asleep in the nights, I locked the doors for no entry because I would have beat them with a stick upon re-entry, the door. It contributed to my nightmares.

This contributed to my nightmares because of what I learned, human contact. I left for days, and my mom came by when I was finished with money to pick me up. I called her and she said, "Okay, honey, I'll pick you up after I get there. I'll call you." "The money she left was great." But it suggested that I should go out and have fun. She never gave me all the gear needed for that day. "When you live in a society like this, your lives should be perfect. Pictures up everywhere stating just what people would do in those situations." It showed a prediction about what came on next on TVs and stations because they put the ads there about video games, Sleeping Man, and ads indicating they could predict. Everything.

I didn't want to be everything. True. I wanted to be lone, take all those signs down. If everything wasn't perfect, far cry was present. She left money on the counter for me. "My mom left money on the counter for me." She left money on the counter for me. "What my mom was doing there?" I was on call and found out what being on call means. I was one phone call from my mom picking up. "When I had a phone call, it suggests that I was seen." I was raised in subjective reality, a place that you feel peace only if you were suggested with enough, ideas that make up your mind. Enough ideas that make up your mind. You should then get a call and be taught about it. "I answered the call." She saw me before behind technology but never came close. She set me up with enough items, TVs, and everything to stay sane. I'd bake them if they ever encountered me. My mom left money on the counter for me. "What are you doing here?" she said. I left money on the counter for her. Why wouldn't I if she did it for me?

"Everybody out."

I sat down. "When I got comfy." Comfy. I thought about sitting down. I was in my house relaxing. I came from the common room. I came from the common room. I went to sit down. Someone sat on the couch before me; it was just before I sat down. I was interrupted by another who sat down just before I sat there. No one was home with me. That was the thing. One sat down on my seat before me.

"'Very body out."

Inspected. "I boarded a ship. I thought about why it was open. It looked like any regular old ship, so I went. I was inspected. I would have been less impressed if I didn't explore it while I was on board, or come close to the ship to see what it was like." After my inspection, I was lying on the bed for quite some time. I looked at the ceiling; I adjusted in bed. I got uneased by it. "I got up to look around and couldn't find my way back to the room I was in." It was too beautiful, so beautiful; the way back wasn't the same as the way through or there.

The lights were on, and it looked like outside from within looking at a light lit panel. The lights were bright, but I was hiding behind a panel. And could only see light from a panel. "I was lucky to have seen it because I was reluctant; I had gotten out of bed." I did a few more seconds of exploring and saw a man dressed in a space suit. "The lights were on under his visor, behind a see-through face shield, that was temper-proof, shatter-proof glass, a space suit. He walked from behind a corner very slowly." His hand was up, and I could not see why. It seemed like he was carrying something. "There was so much peace that I could tell that he wanted me to follow him because I heard his voice in my mind. I got one more look at this man's visor; it looked like a lit light green face from the light, a first-person camera point at him, but it was a light green. I was abducted. I wanted to stay in this remote ship. Abducted." Behind the ship's lights was like it was light out, but it wasn't; it was dark, and lights were on in the ship behind lit panels. Like artificial light out behind binds. Behind lit panels, it looked like it was night out. It was night out like light hit panels. It was light lit panels, and I remember getting ready for Halloween. I continued anyway. I thought Halloween. I did, picking up stuff and putting them away, where no Halloween was.

Deep space.

Everybody out!

"Everybody out!" The captain shouted. There were cops on a hill pulling people over. People were driving slowly past this traffic stop, and ever more slower as and after they were pulled over. People were being pulled over because there was a traffic stop. "And it was fixed. It was fixed because the cops were pulling people over and made it so. It was funny because cartoons lived in a fixed environment. It was a two-dimensional, holding everything together, a picture fished out of the mind and frozen in time shows this two dimensional, a bungalow, a station. Glue. Holding it together, things the mind noticed it was so that it was held together. If you couldn't see it, it was just further in, not around you like being in 3D. Just beyond the two-dimensional, down the street who came from a park nearby, another police cruiser was parked nearby, behind the two-dimensional on the same highway that showed the two-dimensional, but this cop was from a three-dimensional just down the street behind the two-dimensional.

Everything you could imagine about 3D life states just what a three-dimensional is. "Knock on a front door. There was a knock on the front door; while looking into the window, she noticed the knock, her knock, because she was knocking. The knocking wasn't like she was visible." She was seen so she bailed out. "She hit the door frame by accident before she took off. After a few steps in the door way. Before she hit the door frame, she took off." And it was not because of the hidden camera at the front. "If her mind was read, she would take off. She suspected that her mind was read, so she took off because her thoughts aligned with being seen. Being seen she would take off."

There was no knock on the door this time. "Police department." The door was hanging wide open. "You could hear an echo that lasted a long time. Like seconds." It was as though the echo was enchanted like your fairy godmother yelling a scream at the top of her head. The echo was fake. Empty. Unheard. Played anything to show that the echo was an echo. People drunk crashed the house left, right, and centre, looking for nothing, a good time. Partying, they might have slammed into the door worse than the female this time; they crashed the house. They were drunk. They saw nothing. They knew there were hidden cameras throughout the house. And they were always watching. They were stashed in dark corners, in clothes, over your head at the front entrance. You could see from your mind a camera in there too. Much like you can see when you dream. But in reality, you don't have eyeballs in your mind. And from remote locations, furthermore, you have a camera. "And one hanging just outside the front entrance. Just to the officer's right."

You could see the front of her uniform from the view. It was navy blue. "She was hanging on the door frame with her left shoulder on the left door frame, in front of the left door frame, hanging just inside with her gun drawn hanging down by her front waist with both hands holding the gun and a night stick in her right waist." When there was no one there, she took off again, this time suspecting that no one answering was a sign that they read her mind again; she looked. She took off.

"The real reason the people showed up was because of a theme park near the house. The theme park was a medium sized hill, and down the slope. It was like the house was haunted. It wasn't true, but if it were, the slope would whip your face with snow. The very first camera showed one attempting to take over the park a long time ago. You could see a hill, and there was a man attempting to take over the house. "Police department."

'Very body out! "Everybody out!"

I walked into a maze.

"Enchanted hymns."

"I started my imagination." Everyone gathered around and we listened to enchanted hymns in the forest. I got up to hear, "Enchanted hymns." Enchanted hymns, in the forest.

I saw, "A sparkle of imagination."

"I listened to enchanted hymns."

"Sparkle, happens."

Sparkle.

I was looking at gold. Gold. It was gold. I couldn't quite get my hands on the gold. It was like I was clumsy. "It was floating there in my mind. Then I could see the gold sitting there on a counter." I got it in my hand. I got a grasp of it with my left hand, but I went to grab it with my right had but it slipped. I picked it up inside the store. "I then got another glimpse of it near the auctioneer." He saw it. I could tell by the look in his eyes that he was hooked, like the zombie I became when I saw the gold. He saw. He saw. The deal closed. I got another look at it. "I got a hold of it." And it slipped not out of my hand but into my grasp. "Into my grasp." It was mine.

Gold.

Halloween.

"Trick or treat!" Trick or treating. I was trick or treating when Halloween rolled around, and I was thinking while running. Running in Halloween was the name. Name of the game. Halloween. I looked outside and saw the street light light up the corner from within a rotting corpse, a mummy I was standing with. "The trees were smiling orange I could barely see." A wolf howled coming from behind the connotation, behind the house, in my imagination in the story but not in real life. But it was not behind the house the wolf howl came. That line was only there for decoration and so was the howling; it was heard behind the house, all over the place. Halloween ended with a wolves' howl, witching hour. A wolves' howl. "Trick or treat!"

Everybody out!

Nuclear winter, it was getting dark, I could see the sun through the ash, a grey, dim sky. Everything was covered in ash. From my point of view, people were living scarce, clothes packed. I saw in one man's window so they could move. One man's house was like a burning tesla coil. You could hear buzzing; he fried the electricity in the house, creating a portal for himself so that he could escape. "Those who were rich were thankful for all the money they had." And those who don't, at the bottom of society, boom, died of natural causes; they should have rapidly flexed so that they changed bodies. And the fortunate ones pulled the cord for a cure from death. The purgery. Nuclear winter was over just as soon it was on. I felt like death. In the middle of nuclear winter war.

Everybody out.

"War."

"Everybody out!"

Money piled up in a man's hand because he discovered it. He put money there in reality, but it was only two dimensional. When he put money there in his mind, there was no dimension, and because the man put money there, it could not have dimension any other way. He invented the third dimension. He thought about money and wandered up the street. The act of thinking and doing things within the minds spawned things, and even money. The money came from the third dimension, after you wandered up the street, and back it spawned. Saints praised. "Praised." It is unfathomable. Not worthy of a peasant's tale. It was because he discovered money within his mind. He found money at the edge of space, near exospace. "It was not so that exospace made the money from scratch, it was so that time was tired and was copied too many times, such so that it tired out and gave up money at the dispense of the man's discovery. Long time ago there was money."

The discovery of money came about after a man needed money. The man put it there in his mind. The money knew he was good. He could hear the inside of his mind chanting, riches calling to him. The riches were really thinking. It was so peaceful that he could hear his thoughts, like whispering. "In his mind, the money was made. In the beginning there was nothing, so they thought about everything instead of making it." And when it was done it was made, one dimension down, someone thought about it. He thought about it. One dimension down, so it could be conjured, spawned. He felt rich. And a key as to what he was thinking, the money the man put down got him rich from the discovery of money. The man who put the money there knew it would get another rich because he needed it, not wanted it, "One dimension down, he could hear thoughts; he heard the chanting and praise for the likeness of money. Enchanted. The money piled up in this man's hand like magic; he got so rich he had to move it for more money to spawn there. The money piled up like saints singing and dancing and rapping. He started eating every time he saw his money. He was rich now. He talked money. "Talking money."

Everybody out!

The computer got to the destination. It thought, "I knew it was good." The computer reached to that destination because I told it. The computer later put it in the destination. "I thought, I'll start then, and the computer would have to get me rich." I also said. The computers started up. He the computer was signing everyone out because the money was good for signing people out. The computer thought, al right I get him rich. The computer said, "I'll walk on the ceiling and finish the job first then. It is because I'm inside this computer that I'll walk on the ceiling." He responded, "I'll also walk on the ceiling and get the job done." I typed in, "Walk on ceiling to get job done." The computer showed. Right then, since we're in business, I'll just shut this down then. It was talking in his head, just like how I started. I knew because this is what he wrote. He typed in and his reality was objective to the keyboard. He wrote, "Once upon a time I met a man and I got him rich. I walked on the ceiling to get the job done, and I signed him in so that there was nothing on the computer but money to take." Once upon a time. On the ceiling I walked; money talked. I gave money by computer a mouth. The computer walked on the ceiling and gave away money to me; he walked away to get his money that I spent him. I sent him a message. He opened it. I was walking on the ceiling in the clip.

"People live on. There is enough technology for people to live in colonies, throughout space, survival." The war would not stop, so everyone who had knowledge of the war switched sides and got off the planet inhibiting, a future that shows the enemies what to be afraid of." We left them in fear; we left them in a haunted house decorated by scare actors under heavy guard. Scaring the holiness out of them.

Inhibiting a future war.

The future is actually what you are doing at that time, not what is over there. Over there is the past. Things that are there must the past, that they were put there, over there, over there is the past. "They built structures, their minds, so they did not have to do certain things again. Some people have it so rough that they visit a certain location then get to building their time resort." Building time resort. Space time travel.

Doctor Pathic.

A man lived in, a jungle. "Everybody out!" I live in the jungle because of the haziness of time travel. People everywhere made reality look weird, deep space. If you travelled enough, you could probably meet yourself. "You could see a man peeking." It probably won't be a good match, but you might have a suit hanging around, or a couple of good alien bodies from your mind, your own crew. "Then you could dispatch these bodies into multiple stages of reality." Built within traps and resorts so as to keep you from going crazy by meeting yourself. This is how reality started. Beings in your mind from thousands of years ago were then dispatched into multiple stages of space and reality, which made it possible for advanced life.

Doctor Pathic

They were living in space for a long time before even stories existed. Stories existed. A story that never happened; they lived and existed in this non existence, this non-existent story. "Just before the beginning of the universe, a civilization was living in peace, in exospace. They lived near the moon, a moon that hasn't reached the status of the moon yet because it doesn't exist yet. Over the horizon, you could see the moon. And two thirds past the moon's surface was all sky. They lived there in a certain way. They lived in exospace."

They lived in exospace. They called it the beginning. The technology there is always turned on, showing a show, and when you got up to the base, you could tell that this base was advanced, because you could see tech all over, hanging up everywhere, showing protocol, showing trouble shooting. Copies, back engineering hanging up everywhere, it showed what to activate in the event of that engineering copying back. That and AI kept the housekeeping up for advancement that it may need to run across, and it analyzed the dirt it picked up to make a trip back to where this dirt came if met by the needs of the people there. It sounded like a white noise speaker, the fuzziness of space. And these guys didn't need security. "The only way you could intrude was by telling advancing all the time.

The base they lived at wasn't connected to the moon. It was connected to a computer hovering over the moon, simulating a picture on the moon just above it, near the moon. "There was one camera and that was because these people trusted each other and always watched the same spot on the camera, in their places, and were always on time when things were happening, like clockwork in a story that never happened. They were always on time to see if things changed, not that things were noticed to see if it changed. Like if they went there, things would wind back to the same way. Watching it, you wouldn't know that more happened than what you could see. Because they always were doing the same thing on camera, the picture never changed. Just thoughts in their minds changed.

They watched each other, and when they had something to do, they would spend their time caring, and that made a scenario in the mind that we then fished out lest we needed it. They were careful who to watch, and everyone was always right. "The camera showed half the moon base, a crater, and half the sky." Just over the rim of the moon base, these careful beings kept a gun called The Angler, and The Angler was built for time travel, not war. You could not see the gun. Just under the horizon. Their way was so that if they were ever infiltrated, you would know right away. And still, one camera showing the back of one resident's back checking out everything. He should be hopping, but these cameras were like they weren't always right. The people were geniuses. We all had someone watching our backs. One day there was a war, and everyone scrambled because the antagonist was catching up. We were infiltrated from the base down. Someone owned rights to the base and told everyone that it was time to leave. The sirens went off. She said that we got to go, but explained by telling a story.

We boarded a ship, and when we left, I was teleported to earth. "The plan was to repopulate the base without contact and without infection. Because the people in the beginning were perfect." Like Mother Mary. They saw, though, from their minds that they were genius inside, and the others were advanced beings with beings in their minds who had everything right. And on the other side of the base, we all lived there like clockwork and noticed that those people were there for us. We always had a camera at our backs, and we never moved from those spots. We only changed our thoughts. It was always Grey who came to help and took us for regular UFO rides. Grey made everything better. "We hugged Grey for helping and living with us." When we approached the ship, from the distance we could see Grey waving at us at the base of a ship. "He waved and helped us regularly."

Grey.

While I was thinking, I thought about what I saw. A man over there, I thought. I saw. I was thinking. "A party." The other party. The party I was used to. "The party over there." Driving. "They were all driving." Thinking. Driving their cars and tractors. It was me. "It was me. Just me." I thought. It was just me, a bottle and a joke I could barely hear from two other guys over there, not even talking to me. "Tractor." I thought about this because I was there.

While sitting alone, I saw "party. I was at a party. I was at this party because I wanted to drink." This type of party, with a party over there and two drinks, was a party I was at. I was partying for them. "But I wasn't partying with them." The party came from meaning. "I thought." It started out with a ball. I thought. "Party." This joke was very inviting and would break a party for me. I was used to being alone because I was drinking alone, and I was sitting on this seat long enough. I saw a party. The people over there, with their joke, was good enough. The party said, "The party over there." I left. Party everywhere as I was walking through town. I noticed many with a joke they told, and as a joke, many drinks I took, but not for real. "I joked with myself and thought, that was a lot of drinks." I thought that because the party was there. "The city, I caught up on in history."

I got back to my place and caught up on history. I was browsing through the computer when I noticed nothing. "I'd already seen and learned all those subjects already." Each path there was had people at the end of it. But none that I thought about. The path I took was empty. The people at the end of it weren't there. "The path I took had me at the end of it. There must be because the path I wanted to take there was with no one on it." The path took me. I knew what the path had on it. There were no one on it. I learned something new.

"The path I took."

The path I took had dreary motion. Those "Dreary motion" plants were psychoactive! I saw that they were living and that they were singing. The thoughts I had were of what these plants were doing. "I wasn't going to smoke them, but I noticed them from a land that wasn't real." I noticed that this land was only real because of thoughts. "If you had certain thoughts then you were allowed to be." I think this land came first because it has wisdom. Thoughts of madness came first, and visions. Those were the laws of reality. Reality only shows what you need to see, then thoughts of madness to see if that fit. If you went to this land, you had visions. The visions were there to alert you of incoming threats that would harm your body, thoughts of madness came first in reality to protect you when you learned.

Doctor Pathic.

Time travel is everywhere. "The tesseract." It comes from a tesseract. "Tesseract. It is matter from the universe, held together by other atoms, in a neat and puzzling way." Tesseract. You must sit on or use it. Tesseract. If you have the item, it might yield that; you have enough to do certain things again because of the planet's shape. And if you wanted to time travel, build the planet up to a certain weight, like the past happening again. Or take it down to match a certain weight, according to what you would like to do.

You built your mind a certain weight.

Once upon a time, the land comes from a ruined place that was made by the laws of physics. "It was correct to have been made but not necessarily right." It was like the universe came from war, a sudden war." Then there everything was, a giant explosion, a violent giant explosion throwing everything everywhere. "Messy, like it didn't want to eat and said, no!" I never came from the Big Bang; I was made after the Big Bang came about. "It was like we didn't want to be a part of the Big Bang." Or we made it out of the Big Bang and let it by so that we could rule, in theory, in peace. "Or the Big Bang didn't want us part of it. Or like we weren't born in time and we were left to the Big Bang. Like we left the Big Bang cause it was too dark." Or both. Like we came from stasis.

It starts with an experiment. "Picking up tubes and spilling them into flasks." Seeing if it bubbles up to support gas. Scribbling notes into paper results. "Measuring to make sure measurements were correct." I was all alone, theorizing in a makeshift lab. Words to describe it were exasperating. "I saw the experiments." I was making tools, tools out of chemicals. "When the chemicals bubbled up, I took more stabilized chemicals cut into the lighter chemicals until I had acids, then eventually tools, like plasma cutters and flamethrowers and gas in a tube." With it, I could solve problems, like what the chemicals did, and what they will do to certain agents. "Theorizing."

Without the lab, I was stuck thinking metaphysics. It would almost be like war if I was stuck with metaphysics. "Torture, the notes that put you to sleep." I tried brainwashing to myself so that if someone asked and psychoanalyzed everything people have said, it would wear in like I didn't know. "Theoretics changed the world." They were thinking about a successful experiment. I measured right in a lab. "Thinking about the results, I could do it again." In fact, if I did it enough times, I would have enough raw ingredients to make a potion, an elixir, and even magic. "Enough ingredients of one thing would make a potion." If I made an elixir, it would change my intelligence. "If I made a potion, it would change my body. If I made an elixir, it would change the world. If I made things right, magic. Theoretics. A man taking notes is what I see. He is theorizing. In dark, they could see, coming from pages."

I saw. Theorizing, without it we would go mad or face life, an infection, face plague, viruses, diseases, and face death. "In life, if it were black enough, we would become an infections friend." They were theorizing if the smell or look was potent. "If the smell was potent, it was good enough for a deadly chemical." If the look was potent, it was good enough to eat. The picture was of a man peddling. We had sustainable energy. We dug into the ground until we made C4, gunpowder, cutters, cannons, guns, and more. Then the picture was of a perfect land. A functioning village. "If it was rearranged, it would look like a saw just about to cut a person's arm." If we rearranged it again, it would look like a functioning village, and if we rearranged it again, then there would be supplies. Pounds and pounds of atoms of a kind. "Pounds and pounds from a village. Pounds and pounds for war. Village." Villager. "Villages'." Village.

Power of the wind.

A day before the next, today. "People were yelling at the top of their lungs, selling things. They were screaming because they could not hear over the yells." Then some started singing because they could not hear over the screams or yells. Another man played music over the singing, screaming, and yelling. In fact, it was so loud that people started a play up to sell their goods. "Others started a play, and did so while also yelling. Then some said a play and screaming would do. And others, then a play, screaming, and yelling would do." Then some said a play, screaming, singing, and yelling would do. Then another said, yelling, screaming, singing, music, and dancing. "After yelling and screaming and singing and playing and dancing, it was so loud that everybody pitched in and made the world dance. It got even bigger, though."

The people who were not selling things all started a shop fixing things of theirs to make it good. "They were all singing and dancing; they were happy. The village cooperated." The singing, screaming, and yelling went all the way to the stores. But they were bartering, so the yelling, music, screaming, playing, and dancing would not be stopped. In fact, they would not send one home without singing or dancing over the crowd to see if their product worked. They shouted, screamed, sang, danced, played, and yelled all the way to the bank; they were living in harmony, singing, screaming, yelling, and dancing. Screaming.

"Everybody out."

Power of the mind.

Power to the wind.

"Work, properly."

Gadgets.

Everybody out!

Power to the wind.

The organ is hooked up to water and digests. It sucks within the body. "It sucks water." Light must petrify the fluid for it to digest properly. The system's fluid mixes with acids in the stomach. Used right, you digested, or made a weapon with enough muscle.

That must activate your brain, because if I were to say it with definition, their words would dilute your mind, and deep within your conscience you'd know the words were wrong telling you bad things.

Ballad of the wind.

Once upon a time there were creations in the universe. They were created to fuse. They fused because it is right. They fused the land back together from madness, seen in the Big Bang. They fused together the land by digging into the ground then pulling out sediment. They pulled the sediment into gunpowder and C4. This was correct thinking, which is why they fused. In the beginning it were correct to fuse. In the beginning, there was darkness, in the beginning. Molecules are there for change. Even if the body fails, at least you would change.

Everybody out.

"Good luck."

I was dropped off with no food, water, or survival gear. I was listening to broadcasts before I was kidnapped and dropped off in the middle of nowhere. I didn't take any gear. Just my wits and my hands I was left with. I saw them leave, and only had my conscience on me. I was thinking. "I could see my things getting further and further into the wild as the helicopter receded away. I had to think quickly because as the helicopter left, so too did my wits and a picture from my mind." The mechanical copter. A picture from the mechanical helicopter was in my mind. "I saw that I was dropped off through kidnapping. I ran as fast as I could away from the capturers because my imagination was fresh." When I was gone out of sight, I dug into the ground and mixed everything into C4. A gradual mixture of clay, trees, feces, etcetera were whisked together by me. "I took a small chunk, keeping the animals in mind and my surroundings." If I started a fire, it would attract bugs, and they would be burnt alive quickly.

I noticed there was a jaguar near me, so I let him close and saw my radio I'd made from scratch. I talked into it, and when I did, I listened for the jaguar. He was already tame, the speaker said. So I quickly took off after I pressed the radio to have the jaguar even more tame, a radio. "I heard the jaguar talking into the mic of the radio. I ran into my wits again, until everybody heard me. I wasn't making radios out of feces for free. They found me and I asked why." I thought, I'll make something. I found that making something attracts attention, so I ran away again. "I quickly made something." I couldn't make what was in my mind because it turned into a psychoactive plant from harvesting an already used product; my mind picked up a psychoactive plant. So I made C4 in the wild and then took off for this psychoactive plant.

"Imagine that, a psychoactive plant touching your mind." Beware that things in your mind are hundreds of billion trillion million quadrillion miles away. I couldn't see the psychoactive plant anywhere, so I blew up the C4, and when it fused, there was a picture from my mind. A different picture in my mind, not the psychoactive plant. "The C4, I blew up the land until I could fish out the picture, and I fished out this picture out of my mind from reality after seeing radioactivity, eventually seeing enough atoms fusing together." It was a picture of the psychoactive plant, not the psychoactive plant, basically stating that the plant noted from his end that I was to keep the C4 and gunpowder safe with me and the picture.

"We hooked everything up by exploding it again, making technology; the picture I took was a now a back door to technology. I blew up the picture with C4 and realized that the picture was fresh from my mind and so was this back door. I realized that I should make what I saw in my mind. I received a message instructing me to look within the technology on screen. I blew up the land again and made a computer to see a picture of the of psychoactive plant on screen. It was the psychoactive plant waving at me, telling me that I could push a button for his end to fix the psychoactive plant from becoming psychoactive within my mind, so that I could see and to prevent sick images from getting out on TV by using the psychoactive plant."

The picture it gave me was to tear up the entire land for the arrival of a psychoactive plant like the one I'd seen on screen. I had to hop like nine planets to get the one from my mind, and the only difference is how they were born, those psychoactive plants. I saw that I had everything, so I hopped a planet. "The problem with this one was the perception of it; the plant wasn't there." And the one who should have seen the plant there was mean. It states that he destroyed them all. The problem here is that there were no plants like that. I took my technology to see if I was clear for another hopping of the planet. "There were problems, so I fixed them. I took everything and tested these beings for sight, then I gave them advanced technology so that they could learn a hundred times easier, quickly." If I took the old-fashion way, I would nurture them and bring their muscles and mind to life.

This planet was fixed and was even easier to get to my friend the plant. "After I boarded the planet, I just hopped, as I was out of gasoline. So I gathered until I had C4. I mixed the land up again and again until I had C4. I mixed it up until it loosened up gasoline from the spiciness of the C4. That made the gas I needed. I hopped a planet again." And this time everything I needed was there except advanced technology. I was left with a picture in my mind. "I fished it out by making what it suggested. This left me with a picture in my mind." I blew the land up until it made this picture. "It was enough to dislodge what was in my mind." I then started hallucinating; I then realized that the plant was in reality supposed to be there. These hallucinations were just plants moving in wind. I made it. When I saw this plant, it was real in reality and not in my mind now. "I passed by it like I originally wanted to in the first place." Careful not to go insane by taking too much time. I passed a psychoactive plant. I'm sure there are many other psychoactive plants out there left, but this one let me pass a security check so that I may advance in technology.

Reactor.

The smell of fuel burns gas.

Ignite, "In winter."

Winter comes in gas. The smell of gasoline burns it up, winter.

After the fuel comes in, it burns winter.

The smell of fuel burns gas.

It ran away because it is a cartoon. The technology has cartoon written all over the inside of it.

He's a cartoon now!

"The cartoon looked out to see the world. I covered up his head because he would have been lonely without his hat." I was walking and took the cartoon with me. He was thin enough to fit through the air into my mind. "He was walking and took his friend, me. He's a cartoon now." The cartoon said, "Here's the plan: we'll tear up the land and make shelter. Before I could get my gear, I turned around, only to have seen the land was different. "I saw a shadow and what was behind me. I turned around to look at it." There was a castle. "I saw the cartoon's head, and I put his hat on his head like before." It was too hot out, plus I could see the sadness on him. I turned the planet the same shape as it was when I put his hat on before and adjusted the weight of the planet by picking up his hat again and placing it on his head. "He picked me up like a bride and spun in a circle with me in his hands. Before, it was like he was flexing his forehead in sadness because of things. I covered his head with his hat, and he jumped up with glee. He said to me, "Cartoons have unlimited arms, so it was easy to get the project done, no shelter." He said to me because I needed to know, plus it was funny.

The land was empty, so making shelter was logical; the cartoon gathered everything up when he saw me coming. Plus, he said, "I saw you coming from a million miles away, so that's how I knew."

"He thought that being around him was peaceful, so he was peaceful." Cartoons have automatic telepathy, millions of dollars, and peaceful minds. He said, "He's a cartoon now." Someone fired up the reactor on dot B, secondary, and it meant cartoon, but not A. He's a cartoon now. The cartoon thought. Why? Because there were too many things going on. "He's a cartoon now." I covered the cartoon's head and put his hat on his head again. "Put on a cartoon's hat?" I said. I put it on his head. I talked to him for a quick sec. "The cartoon copied me and started talking to me too." What he said, I don't know. I talked to him too. I understood that we were talking. What we were taking about, I don't know. I thought about what we were doing; we were talking. "When I found it, about what we were taking about, I was given an eye." Someone gave me an eye. They spawned a set of eyes, not gave me them.

These eyes talked to me as though they made a noise like looking at something for a long time. They showed me they were eyes, is what they showed me. I wasn't looking at what those eyes were looking at. They peeped at me. "I understood to look away when they did." When they did, I no longer wanted to know what they were looking at because I understood that it was personal space is what I would have seen. If I checked again, I would have got into an argument, so I understood. I looked at him. "I saw him." He's a cartoon now. The cartoon checked his self; he's a cartoon now. The cartoon looked, also thinking about the eyes. The walk went to us. It started running faster while tying his shoes, careful not to let us trip; mind you, we were standing still when the walk started running faster.

"And as far as tied shoes, we copied everything and put it into a secret file, whereafter we saw once, and when we saw once, would be seen again by the walk for his keepsake." He walked away to finish his walk. We walked for a went. "It was to check on the gold." We walked for a went. We went for a walk. "We walked for a walk." That was the secret way to the gold. I jumped into the mine where the secret gold is. I started golding the mine and outing the stake where mine the gold was. I walked for a walk and found out the real gold was there and in my head. In my head for the peace and in my hands the gold. It was right to buy what you saw in your head; that's how to keep the peace. And when you ran low, show your peace in your head by doing the thing, mining. We ran over there to get the gold after we mined. And that was after we mined. We did it.

Everybody out.

We mined after mining. Then, "We checked on the gold." I checked on the gold. "I walked for a walk." I spent gold. Gold was gold. But it wasn't me, so I bought what I thought about so that gold can see what kind of person I am. The gold said. The gold did. I had gold in my hand. I mined gold. I did gold by mining gold. I gold got. The gold got me. I am a prisoner to gold.

The gold got me.

Everybody out.

Just outside the reactor. The gold was waiting. Eternity brought the gold. I was wandering, telling my fortune. I saw. The gold got me, unlike how I got the gold. The gold showed when I bought my mind. I bought the things I was thinking about. Then gold showed at my door. I used my scooter to get the gold. It was a gold bullion. I later saw while checking out all electrical phenomena that gold brought me. It was so because the gold bought the signal coming from my scooter. He the gold brought me. The gold told me to tell you that I got gold. I got gold.

Gold.

Doctor Pathic.

The gold got me. There is a tournament.

The gold took off to the tournament. I followed and got ready. The tournament was showing it was full and people were there. The gold walked up to the tournament and he said to the gold, "Get comfy." The tournament said, "I'm getting comfy too."

I watched tournament take his seat. Then he was gone, and there was no tournament. Tournament took off. The tournament hid; when you saw right, his feet were sticking out from behind his hiding spot. He waited for the tournament. Then left. Wandering all the time until the tournament was over. The tournament wanders. The tournament secretly picked up the shoes sticking out from a hiding spot. There is magic.

The tournament wanders.

The tournament wanders because there is no tournament.

They signed up at the tournament.

There was no tournament.

They fought over nothing, and I gave them gold to stop fighting.

One of them mined for more when I gave the gold away.

The other kept the secret in his head, his mind. The gold was for luck. He kept it down in the basement. He kept gold. He kept luck. He looked down in the basement and saw he had gold. He kept it for luck. The gold he kept was from his mind. The picture was that he was in dire need for gold. He was seen and left. The gold got him.

The gold said there has got to be a start, a start to the beginning.

He was doing business. He started with gold, black gold. The gold was black and shiny; you saw no yellow except for when you thought yellow, a tiny tinge of yellow was coming out of eternity, you see. Black gold.

"Everybody out."

Everybody out.

"You see."

You see.

The sad Doctor it was in. They were going to make a journal about a haunting when something picked up the paper.

www.ingramcontent.com/pod-product-compliance
Lightning Source LLC
Chambersburg PA
CBHW080453030726

47592CB00011B/3093